The Super-secret Diary of

HOLLY

HOPKINSON

of utter
chaos!

BOOKS BY CHARLIE P. BROOKS

The Super-secret Diary of HOLLY HOPKINSON

Just a touch of utter chaos!

CHARLIE P. BROOKS
and KATY RIDDELL

HarperCollins *Children's Books*

First published in the United Kingdom by
HarperCollins *Children's Books* in 2022
HarperCollins *Children's Books* is a division of HarperCollins*Publishers* Ltd
1 London Bridge Street
London SE1 9GF

www.harpercollins.co.uk

HarperCollins*Publishers*
1st Floor, Watermarque Building, Ringsend Road
Dublin 4, Ireland

1

HB ISBN 978-0-00-832816-0
PB ISBN 978-0-00-832821-4

A CIP catalogue record for this title is available from the British Library.
Typeset in Stempel Schneidler Std 12.5pt/18pt

Printed and bound in the UK using 100% renewable electricity
at CPI Group (UK) Ltd

MIX
Paper from
responsible sources
FSC™ C007454

FSC
www.fsc.org

This book is produced from independently certified FSC™ paper
to ensure responsible forest management.

For more information visit: www.harpercollins.co.uk/green

To Ann-Janine

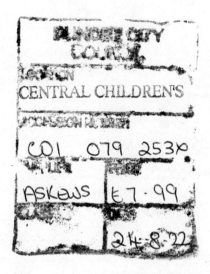

CHARACTERS

HOLLY
HOPKINSON ➩

⬅ VINNIE

DAD ➩

⬅ AUNT
ELECTRA

HAROLD

MUM

HARMONY

DAFFODIL

GRANDPA

PROLOGUE

―――※―――

THIS IS VOLUME III OF HOLLY HOPKINSON'S
OFFICIAL MEMOIRS - TRYING
TO RECORD THE LIFE AND TIMES OF
MY DYSFUNCTIONAL FAMILY.

We are still macarooned* in the middle of flipping nowhere (Grandpa's farmyard near Lower Goring) since Dad lost his job in London, and my parents kidnapped me and my DOOFUS brother and sister.

I am OFFICIALLY waiting for social services and a TV camera unit to come and find me, but if they're anything like the drivers from the Amazon, I'd better not hold my breath any time soon.

> * MACAROONED – stuck in a remote place somewhere that looks a bit like a biscuit.

The village has actually become quite famous since Dad put his excessive screen-time TV watching to good use and turned our pub, the Chequers, into a bistro eating experience. But not always for the right reasons.

We have my swaying Aunt Electra from Bohemia, thank you very MUCH.

She is now OFFICIALLY general manager, generally managing to cause trouble. And, with both Dad and Aunt Electra in charge of the mismanagement, it's losing money faster than all of Grandpa's horses.

So Dad has now agreed to stop being a 'doofus' celebrity chef, but Aunt Electra is still putting spanners in the works of the Village Cultural Events Organising Committee (VCEOC).

Although I am officially attending the Lower Goring village school, I have a double-whopper full plate in my lap when it comes to keeping my family on the rails, as they say in the WILD WEST.

HOLLY HOPKINSON
(BAND MANAGER INC.)

HOLLY HOPKINSON
(RACING MANAGER)

HOLLY HOPKINSON
(FILM LOCATION AND
PLACES INC.)

But I am looking to expire* myself.

So my main holiday job at the moment is managing The Cool, the traumatic band in which my GOOFY brother, Harold, is lead singer and drummer. Things have not gone smoothly for The Cool – even with the assistance of my sister, Harmony, who writes tragic songs for Harold and Stickly, the other guitarist.

* EXPIRE – go up in a large puff of smoke.

Harmony is still as keen as mustard on protesting with social-media friends she's never met, when she can find something suitable to get outraged about that doesn't get in the way of her being boggle-eyed in love with Stickly, or happen when it's raining.

My mum, Sally Hopkinson, is now a **FAMOUS PR GURU** who computes* to London spit-spot fashion. She's also a bit of a handful when she gets the wind between her knees. Particularly when she's orbiting round Mrs Smartside on the Village Cultural Events Organising Committee and going chin to chin with Mrs Chichester, Chipping Topley's worst and only interior designer (and mother of my OFFICIAL countryside best friend, Daffodil).

Dad is not a big fan of Mrs Chichester's shop. He says, 'Just shoot me if I ever buy a scented cushion off that ghastly woman.'

Pardon my French.

* **COMPUTES** – think hard on a train.

Aleeshaa is my OFFICIAL London best friend, but she hasn't been a very good one since my parents **KIDNAPPED** me to the countryside; but she is dead cool, so I'm giving her another chance.

Secretly – and obviously I don't tell Daffodil this – I want to be a cosmopolitan like Aleeshaa and drink cocktails with cranberry and lime juice in them.

And I've forgiven her for not answering any of my messages because she keeps losing her phone.

My dad's father, Grandpa, is RATHER GOOD FUN. The one thing, however, which is a bit fishy about Grandpa is that he keeps the attic locked and says a headless ghost called Mabel lives up there who is very cross. So we all know he's just making that up – but we're not sure why.

Mum says he's a **DARK HORSE.** which is, quite frankly, ridiculous. I think she means he 'has' a dark horse, which is true – Le Prince.

Grandpa is pretty cool about us **INVADING** his farmyard to live in, possibly because all he really cares about is watching horse racing on TV. I am now his horse-racing manager since I appointed myself. His other horse is Declan, who has personality issues that my OFFICIAL animal best friend Vinnie and I need to sort out.

Vinnie is also in line to be one of my OFFICIAL other best friends if he plays his cards right. He's the grandson of Vera, who comes from the north. Vera and Grandpa are dating (although Dad says they're both too out of date to be dating). She mainly washes and irons Grandpa's underpants and bakes cakes that Dad says could have wiped out the Charge of the Light Brigade.

Vinnie is NOT what you would call an academic type. But he CAN talk to animals, which is COOLENDO. as they say in Azerbaijan.

You should know that Grandpa's farmyard is basically an open-air bog (that's a bathroom with no bath in it if you're an American historian). There are animals wandering around, doing stuff whenever they feel like it.

OFFICIAL NEWS ONLY FOR PEOPLE FROM ABROAD

in case you were away when Volumes I and II were finally found in the biscuit tin, you won't know that I have special MAGIC POWERS thanks to the MAGIC POCKET WATCH that dotty Aunt Electra gave me when I was ten years old.

It's been handed down the female side of the Hopkinson family since some bloke called Thomas Mudge got BOGGLE EYES with our ancestor Ethel in 1760.

She was playing the piano for George III at Windsor Castle every night – because that was her job, OK – but he was fed up with listening to Handel's stuff. So she hypnotised the Master of the King's Music and played some modern music from New Orleans. And, even though it was American and they were **REVOLTING***, it cheered the king and Queen Charlotte up no end.

So that's how it all started. If I swing my **MAGIC POCKET WATCH** in front of someone's nose, backwards and forwards, forwards and backwards, and repeat:

* REVOLTING – a bit smelly and not very good at English.

'SPIRO, SPERO, SQUIGGLEOUS SCOTCH,
CAST YOUR EYES WHITHER MY WATCH.'

I can hypnotise adults and get them to do ANYTHING I flipping well want them to. EXCEPT it isn't quite that straightforward. Because sometimes what I intend to happen doesn't, if you get my drift.

Aunt Electra keeps trying to explain it to me – and bangs on about 'it must be for good or fun . . . or there will be unintended consequences' (whatever they are when they're at home, not minding their own beeswax).

BUT THE FACT REMAINS –

SOMETIMES IT

GOES WRONG.

CHAPTER 1

THE BOMBSHELL

SO MUM DROPPED A FLIPPING DOUBLE-WHOPPER CANNONBALL ON US THIS EVENING, THANK YOU VERY MUCH.

She has been on top of the world since the world-famous film director Steven Speedberg snapped her up to be his PR guru while he was making *Black Beauty* on Vince's farm next door.

But when Mum finally skidded to a halt, looking like the bee's knees when she got home from 'the Big Smoke', I knew something was up.

'Is everyone home?' she shouted in her 'bossy' voice.

'I've got **SOME NEWS**.'

'Well, excuse you . . . haven't we all when we can be bothered to be at home?' I muttered to no one in particular – although Barkley was the only one listening in case I was offering steak.

Grandpa was watching the replay of that day's horse racing. So, although he was 'home' in the technical sense, good luck to anyone wanting to do human interrelations with him.

Dad had actually got back from the Chequers just before Mum landed. As he seemed to have ants in his pants I think he's ALSO planning to announce some **BIG NEWS** himself, but he isn't doofus enough to clash with the PR monster machine that is my mother – he'd end up looking like one of those pheasants you see squashed on the side of the road if he tried to pull a stunt like that. So Dad was keeping schtum.

Harmony was curled up like Moggy, our 'excessively impertinent' cat, in one of Grandpa's exploding armchairs, humming some **CALAMITOUS** lyrics to herself.

Harold was making a mess in the kitchen and, as Dad says, 'managing to appear quite intelligent at the same time as being a complete numpty'.

I just can't get my head round how that works. I suppose it might be like pretending to do *The Times* crossword?

Vera, Grandpa's pants-ironer, was hanging around like she does, even though she'd sorted his underwear out hours ago. She sticks to Grandpa like a **BARNACLE**.

So there was a full condiment* apart from Aunt Electra, who was probably doing some bohemian gallivanting stuff in the Chequers.

'We're all ears,' Dad told Mum once Harold had extracted his head from the microwave oven (never try this with anyone's head).

* CONDIMENT – herd of Hopkinsons.

'Well, it's all very exciting,' Mum announced in her 'guru' voice.

'This isn't, like, some SWOT* thing again, is it? Because it's, like, sooo basic and I'm sooo, like, not doing it,' Harmony said from her armchair nest.

'DON'T BE RIDICULOUS, HARMONY,' Mum said.

'WHATEVA, MAN,'

Harold added in his 'ROCK-AND-ROLL' voice.

'EVENTS, DEAR BOY, EVENTS.'

'Just listen for one minute, will you? This is very exciting . . . and an amazing opportunity. OK, so I've been offered the job of EXECUTIVE DIRECTOR OF PR worldwide for *Black Beauty*.'

* **SWOT** – actually means 'Strengths-Weaknesses-Opportunities-Threats'.

Mum's eyebrows did their thing and took off into orbit in opposite directions.

'WELL, THAT'S **FANTASTIC**, SALLY,' Dad said.

'Amazing . . . well done. You deserve it. Isn't that **GREAT NEWS,** children?'

'DOUBLE-WHOPPER hurray, Mum! I can't wait to see Mrs Chichester's face when she hears about this . . . and Mrs Smartside's!' I cheered.

'That's, like . . . sooo cool, Mum,' Harmony purred.

'Events, dear boy, events,' said Harold. Normally he gets a 'shut up' for that, but we were all excited for Mum – except Vera, of course, who just sniffed, and Grandpa, who hadn't heard a word Mum had said.

'Thanks,' Mum replied, using her 'PR' voice – which means you know you haven't heard the whole story.

'The thing is . . . their main office is in New York.'

CHAPTER 2

AUNT ELECTRA'S PEP TALK

AUNT ELECTRA CAME TIPTOEING UP TO MY
BEDROOM FOR ONE OF OUR LITTLE CHATS
WHEN SHE GOT BACK TO THE FARMYARD.

'How's my little town mouse?' she
asked as she came in, whiffing nicely
of sweet stuff like candyfloss and
MARSHMALLOWS as usual.

Aunt Electra has been my
soulmate since the family
Hopkinson was shipwrecked
(in a non-sea way) upon the
rocks of Lower Goring – my
lifeline in the troubled seas of
the Chipping Topley area.

16

'Haven't you heard the news?' I asked. 'We're about to be cast adrift AGAIN . . . and, if you think Chipping Topley is the back end of nowhere, try flipping New York, thank you very much.'

'What are you talking about, Holly?' Aunt Electra asked.

'Excuse you . . . someone must have told you. Mum's been offered a job in New York.'

'NEW YORK?'

'Yes . . . and you don't need to be a mathematical abacus to know it isn't anywhere near York.'

'Well, that's a bit of a turn-up for the books . . . and a full circle in a way,' Aunt Electra mused, not sounding alarmed enough by a long piece of chalk.

'WHAT DO YOU MEAN "FULL CIRCLE"?'

'Oh . . . well – don't you remember? – when I was a little bit younger than you, your Grandma Esme – who was my mother, of course – and Grandpa took me to New York for a couple of years.'

'THAT'S A **FLIPPING LONG** HOLIDAY.'

'WELL, IT WASN'T REALLY A HOLIDAY . . . **MORE LIKE A MIGRATION.**'

'DAD'S NEVER MENTIONED THIS EITHER.'

'NO. HE WAS SENT BACK TO ENGLAND BECAUSE HIS CHEST COULDN'T TAKE THE AIR.'

'POOR DAD.'

'Hmmm . . . well, as you're about to find out, New York is an exciting place, but they do speak in riddles, like, "Have a nice day, sir," which really means, "Go away." And, "Is there anything else I can get for you, sir?" which means, "If you don't give me a huge tip, you can get it yourself."'

'That sounds worse than trying to have a conversation with Vinnie.'

'And they get their words muddled up. Some man told Grandma Esme that he liked her pants, so she knocked his block off.'

'How did he know what sort of PANTS Grandma was wearing?'

'He didn't. In New York they think trousers are called pants.'

'So why were you all there if you weren't on holiday?'

'Well, of course Grandpa was trying to be an artist, so he painted some of the time . . . and Grandma and I used to hang out in clubs where she sang, sometimes all night.'

'Aunt Electra . . . I'm beginning to get the feeling that you are kidding me,' I said.

I know what my aunt's like when she starts telling one of her stories.

'Let's not worry about it now, Holly,' she replied – and off she popped to find something to eat in the farmyard for her breakfast.

So I have got a lot of thoughts crashing round my head like fireworks that some DOOFUS LUNATIC has let off indoors – and there was me thinking that life around Chipping Topley was close to the edge of civilisation.

THINGS COULD BE ABOUT
TO GET A LOT **WORSE** –
THANK GOODNESS
I HAVE MY

MAGIC POCKET WATCH.

I sent Aleeshaa, my **OFFICIAL** London best friend (albeit slightly demoted at the moment), a text to alert her.

HI, ALEESHAA 😵😵😵
I'M OFF TO NEW YORK FOR MAYBE EVA
BEEN GOOD KNOWING U HOLLY

She came back to me pretty quickly, so I guess she's found her phone and been waiting for me to get in touch.

HEY, HOL
THAT'S RANDOM. GO GIRL
GOT TO RUSH AS I OFF
TO MY THERAPY SESSION. 😵

How **COOL** is that? Aleeshaa is already in therapy!

CHAPTER 3

THE MORNING AFTER THE NIGHT BEFORE

BY THE TIME THE CHIEF EXECUTIVE OFFICER OF HOLLY HOPKINSON INC. (THAT'S MY COMPANY THAT OWNS ALL MY OTHER COMPANIES) GOT DOWN TO BREAKFAST, MOST OF MY BIRDS HAD FLOWN. MUM HAD CAVORTED OFF TO HER LONDON COMPUTE 'DRESSED LIKE SHE MEANT BUSINESS', ACCORDING TO DAD.

'You've been to New York, haven't you, Dad?' I asked in my 'all-innocent' voice.

'HAS ELECTRA BEEN TALKING TO YOU, YOUNG LADY?'

he replied.

'I've been looking on my iPad, and it seems to have a very nice park,' I persisted.

'Nice park? Nice for what?' said Dad in his 'snappy' voice.

Dad seemed quite upset as he buried his noggin in Mrs Beeton's cookery manual, so I decided to zip it, lock it and stick it in my pocket.

Harmony appeared, looking like she'd just slept backwards in a hedge. 'This New York thing is just, like, sooo not OK . . . It's, like, sooo basic . . .' she protested.

And, of course, she was right because she will never, ever, ever see Stickly again if she has to move to New York, so it WILL NOT be a *good* move for her.

So I got my **MAGIC POCKET WATCH** out and had a little chat with my elder sister.

'Harmony . . . look at my **MAGIC POCKET WATCH** . . . It goes backwards and forwards, forwards and backwards . . . see?'

'LIKE . . . THAT'S
SOOO BASIC.'

'Indeed . . . now listen to me very carefully . . .

SPIRO, SPERO, SQUIGGLEOUS SCOTCH,
CAST YOUR EYES WHITHER MY WATCH.'

I gave her 'not particularly resistant head' three doses of the verse.

'Harmony . . . you're going to be very sad if you and Stickly have to break up your **BOGGLE-EYEING** when we move to New York, aren't you?'

'LIKE, YOU'RE **SOOO** RIGHT I AM . . .'

'So I suggest you set up one of your protest camps in the farmyard for Mum to see when she flits home from London . . . although don't invite all those other whiffing social-media friends you've never met before this time.'

'Like . . . that's sooo right . . . You're on it, Holly . . .'

'**Excellent.** Harold might also be persuaded to join you. I, **unfortunately**, have to go and see a man about a dog, so Bob's your uncle . . . and best of luck.'

'I'M, LIKE, **SOOO** ON IT . . .'

Harmony confirmed.

25

But, before Harold evacuated his scratcher (the bed that Harold shares with lots of bugs) and gave me a chance to nudge him in the right direction, Grandpa officially announced it was time for his racing manager (me) and him to go and visit the horses at trainer Vince's farm.

We were greeted by Vinnie, Vince's nephew; formerly an unknown monosyllabic rural urchin in Lower Goring, but now my OFFICIAL animal best friend and expert rider of Grandpa's horses, Le Prince and Declan.

But, since **I** got him the job of being the stunt rider in Steven Speedberg's blockbuster film *Black Beauty*, Vinnie is showing signs of getting his cart in front of his horse.

'All riight?' Vinnie asked, making no eye contact as usual. He must get sick of the sight of his shoes.

'I've got some **BAD NEWS,** Vinnie,' I said in my 'manager's' voice as soon as Grandpa had gone off to pat Le Prince. 'We're moving to New York . . . for ever.'

I was hoping that Vinnie would share my misery with me, but all I got was, 'All riight,' in his 'thoughtful' voice.

But then to my amazement Vinnie burst into a flurry of words.

'DECLAN'LL BE SAD.'

I know Vinnie is Vinnie, but I was hoping for some sort of sobbing breakdown on his part – but

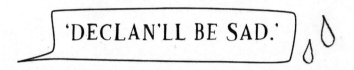

NO.

'Is tha 'n Hollywood?' Vinnie then asked – and I could see where he was going with that one straight away.

I know the film business is ruthless, but I never thought that I would just be a contract negotiator and a suit to Vinnie. Oh, life is a **CRUEL** bowl of chopped liver.

I was NOT in the mood for picking up some scraps of solace from Declan, so I decided to go and find Daffodil. She is a sensitive creature – although hard in the middle – and she will be **DEVASTATED** that she is about to lose her

best friend.

There was, however, a price to pay for delivering such a shattering blow to the unsuspecting Daffodil – I was going to have to visit her mother's shop!

I have tried to shield my memoir readers from the full horror of Charmian Chichester's interior design shop, but it now appears that you and I are embarking on a long and cruel journey. We might as well start in the embroidered-candle department of her shop as anywhere else. It does not have a nice stink, thank you very MUCH.

So I was trying to hold my breath as I gave Daffodil the *CRUSHING NEWS.*

'Daffodil . . . I'm not sure how to break this to you . . . but . . . well . . . the thing is . . . I am going to live in New York . . . probably for ever,' I gasped, running out of breath.

Daffodil blinked a bit – and I knew there was the possibility that she might faint – but all she said was, 'That means you're going to miss Bossy Bossom and Slinky Dave's wedding. Don't tell anyone because it's a secret. Isn't it exciting? I think I'm going to be a bridesmaid.'

Well, you could have knocked me over with a flying bouquet from five paces. It was just TYPICAL of my teacher to nick my thunder from under my feet on the day that I had such **HUGE NEWS** to give Daffodil.

And I can't believe that **I'M** the last to hear about this – spit-spot DOUBLE-WHOPPER annoying,

thank you

very much.

CHAPTER 4

RENDITIONS*

HARMONY'S NEW YORK PROTEST CAMP WAS REALLY LOOKING GOOD WHEN I GOT BACK TO THE FARM. I THINK EITHER GRANDPA OR AUNT ELECTRA HAD BEEN GIVING HER SOME HELP BECAUSE SHE KNEW ALL ABOUT US HAVING TO GO THROUGH ELLIS ISLAND BEFORE WE'D BE ALLOWED INTO NEW YORK.

She'd made some DEADLY banners.

THE HOPKINSONS SAY **NO** TO ELLIS ISLAND!

* RENDITIONS – auditioning potential band members and then tearing them to pieces.

And the one I like best:

> ## HOPKINSON
> # NOT AOPKINSON

That is VERY clever of Harmony – she knows that if your surname begins with an A you go to the front of the queue on Ellis Island, and that's where she's got the idea from. So Mum has a bit of a surprise waiting for her when she comes pirouetting down the drive.

But you WILL NOT GUESS what that DOOFUS Harold Hopkinson is doing today with Stickly.

They're renditioning new band members – today of all days, THANK YOU

VERY MUCH.

If you believe in reinventing carnations, I think we can assume that in his former lives Harold was:

1. Head gardener and busy hoeing his lettuces while it was raining flipping hard, and Noah was knocking up the Ark (quite a long time BC).

 2. In charge of recruiting gladiators to battle themselves to pieces in the Colosseum when Rome was being burned by the Great Fire (AD 64) and probably complaining that global warming was melting his sunblock.

3. Chief designer in a chocolate space rocket factory.

I went stomping into the recording shed with my hands on my hips so that Harold knew I meant business.

'Harold . . . why aren't you supporting Harmony?' I asked.

'Events, dear boy, events . . . Chill out . . . **THE COOL** are going to straddle the pond. We're going to make it on both sides of the Atlantic. Hey, meet Shovel. He's signed up – locked and loaded – as our new band member.'

 Shovel was a hairy creature with the stuff growing everywhere – masses of it on his head, but even more coming out of his nose and ears.

'Hey,' he said in what I assume is his 'rock-and-roll' voice.

'And WHAT exactly do you do?' I asked in my 'band manager' voice.

'YEAH . . . NICE ONE.'

My eyeballs did what Mum's eyebrows do when she's being weird and **CRAZY** – I think that is genetic confirmation that a stork didn't drop me off – and I made noises about me having final contract decisions around this recording shed.

'YEAH . . . NICE ONE,'

was Shovel's response again.

Anyway, the plates that are the spinning world of Holly Hopkinson were revolving fast round my head and smashing together.

A text message arrived from Daffodil Chichester.

'HI, HOLLY ☉ ☉ FELICITY SNOOP AND I ARE GOING TO HAVE PRETTY 💥 PARTS IN BOTTY BOSSOM AND SLINKY DAVE'S WEDDING 🍰 AND U WON'T AS U ARE GOIN TO NY – SO IT'S PROBABLY BEST IF FELICITY AND I ARE BEST FRIENDS AGAIN – HAVE A GOOD JOURNEY 🚤

Well, talk about dancing on my flipping grave, thank you very much.

EXCUSE YOU. BIG MISTAKE … HUGE … I AM GOING TO BE AN INTERNATIONAL PLAYER, THANK YOU VERY MUCH, ON BOTH SIDES OF THE ATLANTIC.

I replied without using any stunted words or emojis.

I was furious, absolutely FURIOUS,

so I went to see Dad in the Chequers to cool off and find out what his **BIG NEWS** was that he hadn't told us.

But, when I got to the pub, guess who was there, not minding themselves in public?

YES.

Bossy Bossom and her intended, school bus driver Slinky Dave.

I thought, *Here we go. Me and my* **MAGIC POCKET WATCH** *can 'kill two turkeys with one of Vera's Christmas puddings', as they say in Lithuania.*

It wasn't going to be the first time that I'd done a multiple-people **SPIRO, SPERO** session – I just have to add a couple of verses.

So I was thinking that, if my **MAGIC POCKET WATCH** instructs them to make me bridesmaid of honour AND tell them to have their reception in the Chequers, Dad and I would have official business preventing us from leaving the Chipping Topley area, thank you very much.

THAT'S THE WAY I ROLL.

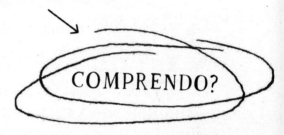

COMPRENDO?

Anyway, just as I was about to **DOUBLE-WHOPPER** flipping well pounce, a whole crowd of Mexican Morris dancers invaded the place, and I couldn't get a clean shot at Bossy and Slinky Dave.

CHAPTER 5

MUM'S GRAND ANNOUNCEMENT

WE WERE ALL READY FOR THE BIG SHOWDOWN WITH MUM WHEN SHE TOUCHED DOWN FROM HER LONDON COMPUTE – ALTHOUGH, WHEN I SAY WE, I SUPPOSE IT WAS HARMONY ON THE FRONTLINE – CHICKEN AND BEANSTALK IN FRONT OF HER GUARDING THE BANNERS TO STOP ANY TRAITORS (LIKE HAROLD) CROSSING HER PICKET LINE.

Harmony is chanting, 'H not A,' mostly to herself, although Moggy and Barkley are lending her some moral support; this whole escapade has thrown a big blanket of botheration over Barkley's future – he does not want to end up in quarantine, thank you VERY much. (Moggy is way too smart to fly baggage class in the back of an aeroplane.)

And I was giving Harmony moral support from a safe distance.

EMBARRASSING

Well, I WAS NOT expecting what happened next. Mum and Dad arrived together, holding hands, as if they'd just walked down the flipping aisle with rose petals and rice being thrown all over them. That is something children should not have to witness in daylight or ever – parents are meant to get that stuff over and done with before they have children. And it made me smell a mouse –

HAS MUM BOUGHT DAD OFF?

'What a lovely fire, Harmony,' Mum observed in her 'casual but fake' voice.

39

'Mum has got an announcement to make, children! Holly, where's Harold?' Dad officially shouted.

Well, how should I know where he is? Since when was I the family sheepdog, thank you very much?

Anyway, Harold wasn't far away, and we all assembled in the kitchen SOTTO PROMPTO, as they say in Bulgaria.

'So THIS IS THE **BIG NEWS.'** Mum announced, looking like she'd just slurped a pint of cream from Moggy's bowl. 'I've had a long think, and I've decided **NOT** to take the *Black Beauty* PR job in New York.'

WELL, you could have heard a BISON drop in the kitchen – and the racing results in the background because this official statement had failed to get Grandpa's attention.

'What's gone wrong, man?' wailed Harold. 'The Cool were going to be transatlantic.'

'Your father and I have thought about what's best for our family, and instead of us moving to New York . . . which was a great opportunity . . . I am going to turn the farmyard into a farm emporium.'

'What's an emporium?' I asked. 'Is it like a poor empire?'

'Holly . . . what do they teach you at school?' Mum asked in her 'adult' voice.

'It's a shop, Holly,' Dad said.

'EMPORIUM is the frontrunner as far as the name is concerned, but it could be arcade, I suppose . . . or stores? We'll see,' Mum declared.

Vera, who was poking her ears in while pretending to do some ironing, made a noise like a large cow passing wind; and the look on her face suggested that she'd got a pretty big **WHIFF** of it.

But Harold wasn't the only member of the Hopkinson family to have their nose dislocated all over the place by Mum's **UNBELIEVABLE** decision.

What the **FLIPPING HECK** was I now going to say to Aleeshaa, Daffodil and Vinnie? I mean, I have pinned my colours to that ship setting sail for New York (nowhere near York), and NOW I won't be on it – so I'm going to look like a right shambles, thank you VERY much.

'SO WHAT ARE YOU GOING TO TELL MRS CHICHESTER?'

I said.

'What's it got to do with her? She doesn't even know New York was on the table,' Mum said.

'Er . . . well, I may have mentioned something to Daffodil . . . and you know what she's like. She can't keep anything to herself . . .'

'Excuse YOU! Don't go blaming me . . . I didn't tell her,' I reposted in my 'outraged' voice.

You couldn't make it up, my mother pointing the finger at ME indeed, when she's spinning us round in DOUBLE-WHOPPER transatlantic circles, thank you very much.

Harmony looked a bit stumped too – she certainly wasn't doing victory laps round Vera's ironing board – then Grandpa looked up from the racing results.

'Will you sell the *Racing Post* in your new shop? It's a blinking nuisance going into Chipping Topley every morning to get it . . . and sometimes it doesn't even arrive.'

HI, ALEESHAA, NEW YORK OFF –
HAD OFFER I COULDN'T TURN
DOWN TO STAY HERE 😉 SEE U
IN TOWN. HOLLY

HEY, DAFFODIL, GOOD NEWS –
MUM HAS BEEN PROMOTED ABOVE
THE NEW YORK JOB SO WE NOT
GOING 😊 SURE FELICITY WILL
UNDERSTAND X 🎩

I guess they'll reply in the morning – it's late now.

CHAPTER 6

MISS BOSSOM ANNOUNCES THE WEDDING PLANS

THE CAT CAME SPIT-SPOT DOUBLE-WHOPPER FLYING OUT OF THE BAG TODAY AT SCHOOL, WITH ITS BACKSIDE ON FIRE AND NO SIGN OF A FIRE EXTINGUISHER ANYWHERE.

Of course it wasn't **NEW NEWS** to me because Daffodil had already spilled the **WEDDING NEWS** beans all over me.

'Quiet, children . . . I have some rather amazing **NEWS** for you,' began Miss Bossom.

45

Daffodil was shushing everyone around her as if she was Official Shusher, and doing weird stuff with one of her eyes at Felicity like she'd got some mud in it.

'So, children, I have an exciting announcement to make . . .'

Then Miss Bossom clasped her hands together, cocked her head to one side and looked up at the ceiling like Vera does when she's dusting AND gave a big sigh.

'Dave and I are engaged to be married,' she gushed like a whoopee cushion.

Gaspar, Wolfe and Tiger made stupid noises while Daffodil and Felicity were mustard keen and clapped like crazy, which hopefully hurt their hands.

'I KNOW! IT'S VERY EXCITING ... AND YOU WILL ALL BE INVOLVED.'

That was when my alarm bells started flashing and making such a FLIPPING racket that I couldn't hear myself think! My **MAGIC POCKET WATCH** and I needed to be all over this or I'd be in the same mess as I was in the nativity play. And I am not impersonating any more chickens or ducks, pardon my French.

But the horse had already bolted from its stable and was halfway to Chipping Topley. Miss Bossom's plans were set in concrete and nailed down with reinforced metal by the sounds of what came next.

'I'm delighted to announce that Mrs Chichester has agreed to help me organise everything ... and I think we all know that she is a leading light in Chipping Topley when it comes to fashion and good taste.'

The boys in the back row made some animal noises, so Daffodil gave them a hard stare. But the lightning bolt that nearly knocked me flying across the classroom was Felicity smiling at Daffodil and giving her a thumbs up.

THIS WEDDING IS GOING TO BE

BAD NEWS.

'Oh, Dave and I are making exciting plans,' banged on Bossy Bossom. 'Of course most of it will have to be a surprise . . . but I suppose there's no harm in telling you a few things. After all, the *Daily Chipping Topley Mail* and RoundaboutChippingTopley.com will be breaking exclusives before the big day.'

'Please tell us, miss,' Felicity Snoop begged.

'Well, let me see . . . we're going to release pink doves when I say "I do" to the bishop and Dave.'

'THE BISHOP?' asked Gaspar.

48

'Yes . . . well, he hasn't confirmed yet, but Mrs Chichester is very confident that he'll want to be present.

'DOVES WHITE, **NOT** PINK,'

Vinnie pointed out.

'Well, these doves are going to be specially dyed by someone Mrs Chichester knows in the dove-and-candle business, thank you, Vinnie,' Bossom replied.

NOTE TO SELF: there may be an animal-welfare issue here that Harmony can protest about.

'Will you be wearing a big white dress, miss?' Iris wanted to know.

'Well, of course that's what most normal brides wear, but Mrs Chichester thinks I will look stunning in pink . . . with lots of sequins and flowers . . . although I'll have to be able to get into the carriage.'

'Will that be like a railway carriage, miss?' Wolfe asked.

Miss Bossom laughed in her 'that isn't funny, you stupid boy' laugh.

'Oh no! And this will be quite something . . . Mrs Chichester has sourced a glass Cinderella carriage pulled by four **BLACK STALLIONS**. Lower Goring will never have seen anything like it.'

SHE'S NOT KIDDING.

'WHAT WILL WE DO, MISS?'

Amaryllis asked.

'Oh, Amaryllis, fear not . . . you will all be involved to some extent or other. Two of you will travel with me and Dave in the carriage . . .' And at that point she gave a very obvious nose wriggle to Daffodil and Felicity Snoop.

'The boys will follow the carriage, holding scented cushions, and the girls will carry embroidered candles with a verse sewn on to them all covered with pink rose petals. We're thinking the verse will be:

Even Vinnie made a face like a deflated football when he heard that.

'WHERE WILL THE RECEPTION BE, MISS?'

chirped Crocus.

'Well, Mrs Chichester is considering all options. It needs to be somewhere big enough for the GOLDEN THRONES that Dave and I will sit on . . . before I do my song-and-dance routine from the old days.'

'Ah, music! Yes, well, I may be able to help out on that front, Miss Bossom,' I announced in my 'Holly Hopkinson (Band Manager Inc.)' voice, thankful to be able to get a word in edgeways.

'Oh really, Holly . . . I'm not sure . . .'

'THE COOL will be playing at weddings around the country this spring . . .'

'I don't think that's quite what we're looking for, dear,' Bossom replied in her 'petrolising'* voice.

I was furious – absolutely

 FURIOUS.

* PETROLISING – burning other people's ideas.

'When is it, miss?' Crocus asked. 'Our family are going to the Galápagos Islands to help wildlife.'

'Well, Crocus dear, the date's a surprise at this stage, but I can say it's going to be a spring wedding when the sap is rising, and nature's animal passion is stirring.'

o o o

Slinky Dave was looking like one of Grandpa's cockerels when we came out to get the school bus home. Strutting around, bobbing his head all over the place with his chest puffed out. And whistling like a **LUNATIC** – it was a wonder he didn't start going

COCK-A-DOODLE-DO.

'I suppose you've heard the **NEWS?'** he asked, all casual, as if it wasn't the biggest story to hit Lower Goring since the over sixty-fives' mud-wrestling FIASCO.

'We can't wait,' Daffodil said with so much desperation anyone might have thought she'd been caught short and was desperate for the loo. 'We're **very** excited.'

I would have answered too if I hadn't been reeling from a DOUBLE-WHOPPER nose full of **WHIFF**.

Dave has clearly decided to celebrate the **WEDDING NEWS** day by smothering himself in aftershave like they do with sheep when they've got blowfly.

Give me a lungful of diesel fumes any day of the week,

SIEVE YOU'LL PLAY.

This has been a very poor day for Holly Hopkinson (schoolgirl) and pretty ordinary for Holly Hopkinson (Band Manager Inc.). But Holly Hopkinson (Film Location and Places Inc.) was still in business – after all, Miss Bossom has yet to choose a location for

THE WEDDING OF THE YEAR.

○ ○ ○

Aunt Electra was mixing her daily tonic in the kitchen when I got back from school: raw egg, some red spicy sauce that she calls tobacco sauce and Mr Lee Perring's Worcester sauce.

She chucked the whole thing down in one gulp and then **ROARED** like a distressed donkey.

'AAARRGGGHHH... THAT'S BETTER.'

she said after she'd wiped away the tears from her eyes.

'Aunt Electra, I have a bit of information for you, which I thought might be good for the Chequers.'

'Have you indeed, *ma petite chérie?*' she replied in her 'French BOHEMIAN fruit' voice. *'Et quoi?'*

'This is the deal, Aunt Electra . . . I'm tipping you off that Miss Bossom is looking for a venue for her wedding . . . It's going to be the Wedding of the Year so it will be good for you and the Chequers . . . and Holly Hopkinson (Film Location and Places Inc.) does not need a fee for this information if you hide in the small print that THE COOL are included in the price. But make the small print very small like politicians do,' I gabbled quite fast.

Maybe I need to polish up my sales pitches and get some of those fillip* charts?

---

* FILLIP CHARTS – invented by an acrobat called Phillip to show people stuff.

'Well, Holly, you are a mine of information . . . and quite the businesswoman too,' she replied in her 'thinking' voice.

NOTE TO SELF: when Mum tucked me up in my bed, I took the opportunity to let her in on my secret – PR style.

'Mum . . . would it be good PR if Miss Bossom held her wedding at your soon-to-be-opened farm shop?'

'Farm emporium, Holly . . . WHAT? Miss Bossom's getting married – are you sure? Who on earth is marrying her?'

'Excuse you,' I told Mum. 'Slinky Dave the school bus driver, of course.'

'Oh yes . . . Isn't that nice?'

'It's going to be the Wedding of the Year . . . and she hasn't decided where to have the reception.'

'Well, that would be a bit different, but hey-ho . . . In these circumstances, why not?'

'OK, well, if I put in a good recommendation for you and get you a viewing with Bossy, will you include THE COOL as a sort of resident band that comes with the food? You don't need to tell her till it's too late for her to change her mind . . . like you used to do when you were in PR, REMEMBERO?'

'I did nothing of the sort, Holly. Well, OK . . . but don't tell anyone.'

'MUM, YOU ARE TALKING TO SOMEONE WHO NEVER TALKS UNLESS THERE'S NOTHING TO TALK ABOUT, THANK YOU VERY MUCH!'

I said in my 'Holly Hopkinson band manager' voice.

CHAPTER 7

LIFE GOES ON

THE SILENCE THIS MORNING FROM ALEESHAA AND DAFFODIL WAS EARTH-SHATTERINGLY DOUBLE-WHOPPER DEAFENING ON THE TEXT FRONT, BUT I WAS NOT GOING TO CHASE THEIR ATTENTION – YET.

Vinnie had just finished exercising Le Prince and Declan when I got to the stables.

'All riight . . . still 'ere?' Vinnie asked in his 'not particularly interested' voice.

Yes, Vinnie . . . still here. Alive and well, thank you very much . . . will be for a while actually. Something's come up, as it does in the world of high fiancé, you know.'

'Riight,' Vinnie replied in his 'doesn't sound riight' voice.

'So, how are the horses coming along?' I asked.

'All riight . . . Le Prince gonna be a champ . . . but Declan's Declan . . . you know wha' 'e like.'

And I did indeed – Declan had enabled me to carry off the Chequers Xmas Pony Race. But he has serious personality defects as far as his usefulness as a potential championship-winning horse is concerned. One of which is that he goes to pieces when Chicken, his constant companion, wanders off, looking for worms and grubs.

Le Prince, on the other hand, is champion material – and his dad is called Royal Approval, and 'ma'am' loves 'stock' by Royal Approval. (If you're an OFFICIAL racing manager, you refer to the queen as ma'am and horses as 'stock'.)

So I fear that history might have to repeat itself – like kippers and older brothers. Because the Hopkinson family's financial fortunes have already been bailed out once by Grandpa and me selling High Five to the queen.

But as I leaned on the gate, chewing grass, talking out of the side of my mouth to remind Vinnie I know my artichokes when it comes to horses, my eye was caught by the ten new Olde Worlde houses built at the other end of Vince's field.

It was Bob's your uncle, all thanks to me as YOU will recall, that I got the famous fish film director to build them EXPRESSO. which has saved Stickly's family from the cardboard city in the supermarket car park in Chipping Topley.

o o o

It had been on my mind that they might have named the street after me, so I wandered across the field, minding my own beeswax, to check out Chateau Stickly.

BUT I GOT A BIT OF
A CODSWALLOP SURPRISE.

I'm not sure what the contents of a budding rock star's garden should be – but I was not expecting some sort of overcrowded refuge for garden gnomes.

The flipping things were everywhere. Hovering menacingly over buckets with fishing rods while others were carrying sacks of stuff all over the place – you just wouldn't know what was in them. And digging holes EVERYWHERE – probably to hide the stuff in their sacks – some of them have even got lanterns.

Then, just as I was about to have a snoop through the window, Stickly came dashing into the garden like a bolting hyena.

'NICE GNOMES,'

I said in my 'diplomatic lying' voice.

'They're not mine . . . they're my granddad's. He's mad, he is . . .

BONKERS.'

I nodded, trying to put him out of his pain – after all, we all have dark secrets stuffed under our floorboards.

NOTE TO HOLLY HOPKINSON
(BAND MANAGER INC.):
Don't trust Stickly – he is a deny-er. He's going to be the troublemaker in the band, thank you very much – I have marked my own card.

Anyway, I was wandering home along the back lanes on my own when guess what flipping well happened?

YES.

Mrs Smartside came round the corner with her yapping little lapdogs who all tried to nip at my ankles, thank you very much.

'Oh, hello, Holly. What are you up to? No good, I shouldn't wonder.'

'EXCUSE YOU,' I replied.

Talk about pots calling kettles cats. If anyone was up to no good, it was her and her rampant pack of wolves going round trying to strip everyone down to a carcass – the flipping cheek of it.

'Just been up to the new Olde Worlde houses next to your orchard actually,' I said.

'Oh, those dreadful people! They have no right to be in Lower Goring . . . blocking my view . . . Anyway, I suppose your lot will all be entering Lower Goring's Got Talent?'

'Oh,' I said in my 'changing your tone' voice. 'I hadn't heard about that.'

'No, I suppose not. Your mother has missed the last two meetings of the VCEOC.'

'Well, she's been rather busy . . . you know, with *Black—*'

'YES, YES, WE KNOW ALL ABOUT THAT, BUT THERE ARE OTHER THINGS GOING ON AS WELL. MRS CHICHESTER AND I HAVE HAD THIS BRILLIANT IDEA . . . SO DON'T MISS OUT.'

And with that she marched off like an overpowered dodgem car, her nose stuck firmly in the air. **BAD LUCK** for her that there was a big pile of fresh horse doings – still steaming – that she stepped right into.

NOTE TO SELF: my **MAGIC POCKET WATCH** and I need to think about what we might do to Mrs Smartside – of course it will be for *fun* or *good*. For instance, it would be very *good* for Mrs Smartside to go skinny-dipping in the River Topley every Sunday morning when everyone's arriving for church. Yes – that would be very *good* for her indeed.

I could feel my **MAGIC POCKET WATCH** twitching in my pocket as I imagined it.

However, Lower Goring's Got Talent is **BIG NEWS** – this could finally be the HUGE breakthrough that THE COOL have been waiting for.

CHAPTER 8

THE ATTIC

SO HERE IS THE REALLY ANNOYING NEWS. HAROLD HAS FOUND ONE OF MY HIDING PLACES FOR SECRET ITEMS IN THE BOG FLUSHING DEPARTMENT. THIS IS A SERIOUS SECURITY BREACH AND A DESPERATE SITUATION – AFTER ALL, MY MEMOIRS COULD EASILY HAVE BEEN IN THERE – SO I'M CALLING VINNIE IN TO ADVISE. HE KNOWS THIS PLACE LIKE THE BACK OF ANYONE'S BOTTOM.

'ALL RIIGHT?'

Vinnie enquired on his arrival. Although with Vinnie you never really know whether that is a question or an answer.

'Vinnie,' I said in my 'in confidence' voice, 'when the coast is clear, we need to find a DOUBLE-WHOPPER safe hiding place for **TOP-SECRET** material that I may have from time to time in my possession. But this is a Bogey Club* expedition, so no squealing to anyone. Yorkel?'**

'Yorkel,' Vinnie confirmed. 'Wha' 'bout attic?' he suggested.

On the one hand it was a genius idea because NO ONE goes up there. But on the other it was a DOOFUS idea because there's a reason for that. The flipping door is locked.

'Well, unless you can walk through doors, that may be a little tricky, Vinnie, my old fruit,' I said.

Vinnie gave me a cheeky, sneaky countryside smile and guess what he fished out of his pocket?

* BOGEY CLUB – Vinnie's private club named after his breakfast.

** YORKEL – yes in Bogey Club language.

- YES. -

The DOUBLE-WHOPPER key, no less. There are no flies on Vinnie.

'What about Mabel?' I asked.

'She be all riight,' Vinnie predicted.

We found a torch, got a ladder and ventured through the door at the bottom of the creaking staircase to the attic. I let Vinnie go first because he's more indisposable than me.

It was a good job that we hadn't finished our full-height growing because the opening was designed for the gnomes in Stickly's garden.

'Riight . . . crates will be good 'iding place,' Vinnie advised, pointing the torch at a load of them stacked up in the corner.

They were covered in dust and had a lot of mice POO scattered over them. Maybe **ANGRY** Mabel, the farmer's wife, has been throwing parties for mice?

BUT I DON'T THINK SO.

'WHAT'S IN THOSE CRATES, VINNIE?'

I asked in my 'whispering' voice.

'PICTURES.'

This clearly was NOT Vinnie's first visit to Mabel.

'PICTURES ... WHAT DO YOU MEAN "PICTURES"? OF WHAT?'

'JUST PICTURES,' Vinnie replied.

'SHOW ME,' I instructed.

So he opened a crate and pulled out one of the 'pictures'.

A picture in my book is meant to look like something: a person or a tree or a house or anything really – even one of Vera's cakes if the mind of the artist has gone completely blank while flourishing a paintbrush.

What Vinnie was now holding up was just a load of not-very-well-painted shapes – to be exact, a big mess of paint. The really young kids at my London school used to do stuff like this, and then they'd pin them up on the wall, and they'd all go crinkly before the teachers DOUBLE-WHOPPER forced the reluctant parents to take the flipping things home.

'Why is Grandpa keeping this rubbish up here? Let's try another crate,' I suggested. 'There must be some proper pictures here somewhere.' In the end we looked in three crates and they were all the same – just kids' stuff.

So this is a mystery – why would Grandpa want to keep a load of kids' embarrassing artwork in his attic? Unless, of course, Grandpa has ANOTHER SECRET FAMILY that he hasn't told us about.

So, if they suddenly appear, we'll have to move into the cardboard city that Stickly's family has just vacated in the Chipping Topley supermarket car park.

This farmyard may have serious health and sanitation issues, but it is now meant to be home. I DO NOT want to find that Grandpa has ordered a better family online to replace us . . .

NOTE TO SELF: it's just spit-spot DOUBLE-WHOPPER occurred to me that this Mabel story that Grandpa keeps spinning us is one massive porky pie designed to keep us out of his attic – and away from those pictures that his secret family may have painted. Unless Mabel has turned into mouse poo, which, I suppose, would make her pretty cross!

CHAPTER 9

LOWER GORING'S GOT TALENT

MUM AND I WERE LAST TO ARRIVE AT THE VILLAGE CULTURAL EVENTS ORGANISING COMMITTEE MEETING. THIS IS A HUMILIATING EXPERIENCE WHEN YOU (THAT'S ME) ARE IN CHARGE OF BISCUITS, TEA-MAKING AND SWEEPING UP (ON A NON-LISTENING OR SPEAKING BASIS) – BUT THE ESPIONAGE WORK MUST CONTINUE.

No prizes for guessing why we were late – Mum was changing the layout in what she insists on calling the FARM EMPORIUM – but this chronicler will be sticking to FARM SHOP. (She's changed her mind three times now, and it hasn't even opened.)

'Ah good, Sally, you're here,' Mrs Smartside announced in her 'you're late' voice. 'Attention, everyone! Come on, we've got a lot to get through.'

Because I only do biscuits, sweeping and spying, I don't even get a 'you're late' from Mrs Smartside; even when I'm DOUBLE-WHOPPER flipping late,

thank you

very

much.

If she doesn't start showing me some respect, the chances of my **MAGIC POCKET WATCH** encouraging her to go to church one Sunday with her pants on outside her trousers BEFORE HER SKINNY-DIP are increasing by the minute. If I was a weather forecaster, I would NOT be ruling it out of the *WEATHER NEWS*.

'As you know, the builders have reported that the state of the school roof is much worse than expected . . . It's going to cost twice as much and take twice as long as they originally predicted,' Mrs Smartside announced.

'So the Lower Goring's Got Talent competition needs to raise a lot of cash. Luckily . . . and I think I can safely say this is a first . . . the winner will receive a GOLDEN TICKET to perform at Vincent's music concert, BEASTIVAL.'

Well, you've never seen shock waves like it go round a village hall.

'Boycott, boycott!' chanted some DOOFUS at the back who lives in one of the new Olde Worlde houses next to Vince's farm.

'That ain't right!' shouted someone else out of sight of the biscuit tins.

'Some decorum, ple-eease!' requested Mrs Smartside. 'I know this BEASTIVAL is controversial, but we need to mend the school roof. And a GOLDEN TICKET prize will attract entries from far and wide . . . we might even be on the

EVENING NEWS.'

'Why can't the winner go and look round Scooby's local pet-food warehouse?' the doofus shouted, and half the people in the village hall started laughing.

Sometimes adults laugh at

very BAD JOKES.

'Why don't yoo clear off back ter town whence yoo come frum!' shouted Vince.

'Why don't you learn to speak English?' replied a 'town' voice.

Then the biscuits started to fly.

At first it was the custard creams, but they were followed by a volley of Florentines (from the vicar of all people) – then there was a blizzard of Jaffa Cakes and Bath Olivers going in every direction.

'SOME DECORUM, PLEEEE-EEASE!'

barked Mrs Smartside, but she then got hit by a Jammie Dodger right in the mush.

Someone on the committee who shall remain nameless (Mrs Chichester) returned fire with a volley of flapjacks and got a blast of macaroons back for her trouble.

And, as if all of that wasn't disgraceful enough, the Double Creme Oreos got fired off like hand grenades from the new Olde Worlde houses lot.

I have never seen adults behave SO BADLY in my life – and guess who's got to flipping well DOUBLE-WHOPPER sweep the whole mess up?

YES.

Holly Hopkinson, thank YOU

very much.

CHAPTER 10

MABEL MAKING NOISES?

SO I WAS MINDING MY OWN BUSINESS LAST NIGHT, CATCHING UP WITH MY MEMOIRS. I HAVE TO DO THAT WHILE THE COAST IS QUIET AFTER OFFICIAL LIGHTS-OUT TIME FOR HAROLD AND HARMONY. ANY EARLIER WOULD BE TOO RISKY – THEY ARE IN THE HABIT OF BURSTING IN ON ME DRESSED AS GHOSTS.

Normally I can hear them coming along the **CREAKY CORRIDOR**. I can even hear Barkley walking along there, it's so flipping noisy. Those floorboards have a lifestyle of their own.

But last night was different. I could hear footsteps in the attic, making my ceiling creak. They just went round and round. So I stuck my head under my sheets and flipping well lay doggo.

Then the cold and colder water pipes started to clang – and I thought, *Hang on a minute, that's what Harold does when he's trying to freak me out.*

So I quietly slipped out of my room and scuttled spit-spot down the corridor to his room, which is the closest to mine, to catch him banging on the pipes. But the room was empty.

His bed looked like he was in it – but I know Harold's trick of stuffing a pillow down it when he goes padding about after lights out. So I leaped on to his duvet to flatten his pillow and had the flipping fright of my life – it *was* Harold.

Harold yelled his head off, and that gave me an even worse fright – so I shrieked my head off times two. Then he jumped up like a bawling baboon and woke the whole flipping house up.

I NEARLY HAD A HEART ATTACK.

'WHAT on earth is going on?' Mum shouted as she came along the corridor looking like a spit-spot ghost herself.

'Mum, why have you got yoghurt all over your face and cucumber under your eyes? You look like something out of a **HORROR** movie. YOU could have given me another heart attack if I'd bumped into you,' I said.

'Why aren't you in bed asleep?' Mum asked.

'Someone in the attic woke me up.'

'Don't be **RIDICULOUS**. Holly . . . the door to the attic's always locked. Now go to bed and don't play tricks like that on your brother.'

'Events, dear boy, events,' I muttered under my breath to Harold as I was frogmarched out of his bedroom and back down the corridor to my own room like a criminal.

THAT IS FLIPPING WELL
DOUBLE-WHOPPER
NOT FAIR.

o o o

So the next morning I had a quiet chat with Aunt Electra when no one else was sniffing around. She comes from BOHEMIA where weird stuff goes on, so I think she'll be sympathetic.

'Aunt Electra, there were footsteps and noises in the attic last night. I think it might have been Mabel . . . it was very scary.'

'Really? That's rather odd. She hasn't been out and about for years . . . I wonder what sparked that off?'

'Er . . . it may have been me going up to the attic?'

'YOU WENT INTO THE ATTIC? BUT IT'S LOCKED. WHO GAVE YOU A KEY?'

81

'Er . . . let's just say I know people who have connections. Have you ever been up there?'

'Certainly not. Grandpa doesn't let anyone up there. Does HE know you've been up there?'

'No . . . don't think so. Unless Vinnie told him.'

'Vinnie . . . what's he got to do with it?'

Now I'd **flipping** well dropped myself in it. That's the thing with adults – they always trick you into spilling the beans.

'Er . . . we were just poking about . . . like you do.'

'Well, I would HIGHLY RECOMMEND that you stop poking about in the attic or Mabel might do some poking to you. By the way . . . anything interesting up there?'

You see, that's what adults do – always trying to catch you out – well, Aunt Electra's going to have to get out of bed a bit earlier in the morning to catch me out twice before the kettle's boiled.

'No . . . nothing. Just a bucketload of mice doings . . . but, unless they borrowed Grandpa's boots, it wasn't them making that noise,' I replied to throw her off the scent.

CHAPTER 11

DOING ART AT SCHOOL

THIS MORNING WE'RE DOING PAINTERS
AT SCHOOL WITH MISS BOSSOM –
FOR A FAILED ACTRESS, SHE
KNOWS A LOT ABOUT THIS STUFF.

History of art is good fun because you don't have to do any work. All you do is look at paintings and pictures that Miss Bossom puts up, and then she talks a lot about them and makes it sound way more complicated than it really is.

The best-friend situation between me and Daffodil has not been dissolved yet. But I am using the same tactics that we learned about in history: I'm just pretending that Felicity Snoop doesn't really exist – and, if she does, I'm not admitting it.

For homework, we have to look at pictures of paintings and artists that did them and write what WE THINK of them – I wish I'd listened a bit more to Bossy Bossom now – and Vinnie is going to come a right riding crop here because he never listens to anything.

o o o

Harold had skipped school and was sitting around like a DOOFUS in his bedroom when I got back to the farmyard.

'Hello, Harold . . . why weren't you at school?' I enquired in my 'band manager' voice.

'Events, dear boy, events,' Harold replied.

'Well, here's another event, Harold,' I said, waving my MAGIC POCKET WATCH in front of his nose.

He was looking like such a dopey teenager, I only gave him two verses of SPIRO, SPERO – I think a third might have OVERCOOKED him.

'Harold . . . you are going to help me with my history of art homework,' I commanded.

'Sure, little sis . . . fire away,' he replied in a sort of smirky way that I'd never heard before after I'd cooked someone.

Anyway, I got my book out. The first picture was by someone called Rembrandt (1606–1669). It was of himself – so mirrors were definitely invented by then.

Q What do you know about Rembrandt's background?

Luckily Harold knew a lot about it.

Rembrandt came from a family of tulip growers who were also very good at football. The Rembrandts were so busy when he was a baby that they forgot to give him a first name. Rembrandt didn't have a camera so he used to do a lot of paintings of himself to give to people.

The next picture was of a train by J. M. W. Turner (1775–1851). Unfortunately he picked a very bad day to do the painting – all you can see is smog and pollution.

Q What does this painting tell you about Joseph Mallard William Turner's painting style?

Harold had some inside info on Turner that I think Miss Bossom will be quite impressed with.

Turner was very impatient – hence he didn't wait for the weather to improve before he did his train painting. He might also have been an even better painter if he'd washed his brushes out a bit better – it would have prevented everything looking so smudged in his pictures. Turner was, however, lucky that he didn't suffer from seasickness because he got caught up in a lot of storms when he was out painting. He also bred a lot of ducks.

Next was a **NASTY** picture of a very weird-looking face by Francis Bacon (1909–1992).

Q   What inspired Francis Bacon?

Harold had done him at school too, luckily.

Francis Bacon came from a long line of butchers. His father, Streaky, was frequently in trouble with the police for running across cricket pitches in the wrong clothes.

The last 'picture' we had to write about was by Damien Hirst (1965–¿¿¿¿).

But it isn't a picture of a painting; it's a picture of a flipping stuffed cow with a chicken standing on its back, who was in the wrong place at the wrong time if you ask me.

o o o

BAD NEWS travels fast.

Everyone is outraged that the *Daily Chipping Topley Mail* broke the story about the biscuit fight today. And, as Mum said, 'They seem to have got their facts horribly right.'

'SO WHO DO YOU THINK THE MOLE IS?'

Dad asked.

'Well, Mrs Smartside was like a storm in her own teacup,' I pointed out. 'So she might have named and shamed a few people?'

'*Yesss*, but that doesn't really make sense . . . because the article suggests that she lost control of the meeting.'

'Hmmm . . . I see what you mean. No, it doesn't really make sense,' I agreed in my 'espionage' voice.

CHAPTER 12

HOMEWORK RESULTS

MISS BOSSOM'S HANDING OUT OUR
HISTORY-OF-ART HOMEWORK MARKS
TODAY. I'M LOOKING FORWARD TO THIS.
I SAT BACK IN MY CHAIR AND GOT
READY TO LAP UP SOME GLORY.

Vinnie was first under the spotlight – he was shaking like Declan did during the housing protests.

'Vinnie, I am impressed. I think you have some very intuitive thoughts . . . I particularly like your idea of the contrast between the INDUSTRIALISATION synonymous with the train and the rural landscape that the train is travelling through. Well done, Vinnie.'

What the heck? Where did Vinnie get THAT from? I am going to have to construct an inquiry into this.

Crocus, Iris and Amaryllis didn't have an original thought between them – so no surprise there – but Miss Bossom gave them some nice words to encourage them, I guess. And she was kind to Brian, of course. Then she came to Felicity Snoop.

'OH, FELICITY . . . WHAT CAN I SAY EXCEPT **WELL DONE!** I CAN SEE THAT YOU ARE ALREADY AN ART **EXPERT.**'

EUCH . . . EUCH . . . EUCH. I'd like to know what the Snoop family have got over Miss Bossom. Maybe they hired a private investigator to look into her past, and they found terrible things that they're now blackmailing her with?

If you think about it, it could be anything. Slinky Dave could be in for a **TERRIBLE** shock.

Anyway, I had to snap out of such thoughts as my homework was next up.

'So, Holly,' Miss Bossom said, 'is THIS meant to be some sort of joke? Well, I don't think Rembrandt Harmenszoon van Rijn would have found it very funny. And Streaky Bacon? Really?'

FLIPPING HECK – Streaky Bacon – I'm going to double-whopper barbecue Harold when I see him.

Pardon my French.

Gaspar, Wolfe and Tiger were all sniggering away. Actually, so was the whole class, so I HAD to snigger too and look like I WAS joking to Miss Bossom.

'Any more cheeky homework like this, Holly Hopkinson, and you will be in BIG trouble,' Botty Bossom said in her 'threatening' voice.

So I was not in good humour for two reasons:

1. Harold Hopkinson had deliberately stitched me up, thank YOU very much.

2. My MAGIC POCKET WATCH had failed me.

Harold was looking as pleased as a chocolate bar that wants to eat itself when I got home.

'How did the homework go down, little sis?' he asked in his 'teenager' voice.

'Very well actually,' I said in my 'lying' voice. 'Miss Bossom had no idea about all that stuff . . . I came top of the class.'

I WAS NOT GOING TO LET HAROLD KNOW THAT HE'D GOT ONE OVER ON ME – BUT I NEED TO KNOW HOW TO WORK

THIS FLIPPING

MAGIC POCKET WATCH

BETTER!

CHAPTER 13

THE HOPKINSON CHILDREN'S INTERVENTION

HAROLD AND I HAD TO PUT OUR DIFFERENCES SOMEWHERE ELSE THIS MORNING AS WE HELD A HOPKINSON CHILDREN EMERGENCY MEETING WITH HARMONY IN THE COOL'S RECORDING SHED (FOR TOP SECRECY).

It's SERIOUS.

If Mum makes us three look like Daffodil Chichester by doing naff stuff with her shop, we will be set upon and run out of town and our schools. Harold thinks the kids at his school will hang, draw and quarter him; Harmony thinks she'll be deliberately infested with nits; and I am certain that I'll get the custard treatment*,

thank you

very much!

So our OFFICIAL emergency meeting agenda is:

✖ ITEM ONE – What the flipping heck Mum is going to call this SHOP. So far she has been chucking crazy names around like store, deli, mall, department store, arcade, retail outlet, shopping centre AND, AS YOU KNOW, EMPORIUM. So we have voted and our final decision is SHOP.

✖ ITEM TWO – We are going to demand a no-compromise ban on scented candles and embroidered cushions. And, just to be safe, scented cushions and embroidered candles as well – you can't be too careful crossing your small print out when you're drawing this stuff up.

I told Harmony and Harold that Mum would take this **SHOP NEWS** best from me as I'm the youngest – of course I didn't tell them that I would be using my MAGIC POCKET WATCH to get the job done.

* CUSTARD TREATMENT – it goes straight from the jug down the back of your pants.

CHAPTER 14

DAD'S SHAKE-UP

MY DAD IS VERY PATIENT – HE'S BEEN STORING UP HIS **BIG NEWS** FOR A FEW DAYS. BUT NOW MUM'S PR MACHINE IS PARKED UP IN THE FARMYARD, THE PITCH IS CLEAR FOR DAD TO THROW HIS **DOUBLE-WHOPPER** SHOCK WAVE INTO LOWER GORING.

And this has taken everyone by surprise in the Hopkinson family, except me.

So Dad is abandoning his 'Raw is More' food strategy at the Chequers. It's probably the biggest shock in the food world since some DOOFUS politician told everyone that chicken eggs have salmon in them. Which obviously caused chaos because fish-flavoured eggs were never going to be a winner.

But Dad has had some problems with his 'Raw is More' movement. Three whole coachloads of gamekeepers had to make an emergency stop at the 'terrible service' station on their way home after the pheasant sashimi put a spanner in their works on a riotous scale, and they had some unexpected movements of their own.

'From now on the Chequers will be a floating world food festival,' Dad officially announced to the media.

That's my new friend from the *Daily Chipping Topley Mail* and the woman from RoundaboutChippingTopley.com, as usual.

'We are going to fascinate the palates of our GOURMETS with temptations from around the globe,' Dad continued in his 'barmy' voice. (I think Aunt Electra has had her mitts on this plan. This is probably the sort of stuff they eat in BOHEMIA.) 'So prepare to feast on Kiviak from our Inuit cousins over in Greenland.'

After some DOUBLE-WHOPPER quick research, I found out that Kiviak is a traditional food made from birds that are sewn up inside a seal skin and then placed under large rocks for three months – to keep the smell in! Then it's eaten whenever someone has a birthday or wedding.

Not sure I've tried that before. And – for the record – Dad made the bit up about it being from our Inuit cousins. Unless Grandpa has some **COUSIN NEWS**, I do not have any cousins.

CHAPTER 15

MUM PLAYS UP

SO GUESS WHICH ITEM OF CLOTHING WAS
MAKING ITS RURAL DEBUT WHEN I GOT
BACK HOME TO THE FARMHOUSE?

YES.

MY MUM'S SKIN-TIGHT LYCRA
BOTTOMS. OR ELASTIC-POLYURETHANE-
FIBRE BOTTOMS AS THEY SAY IN
CELLULOID VALLEY*.

Mum had been to 'a class' at the village hall. But I'm not sure what they learn there because she didn't have a drop of sweat out of place.

> * CELLULOID VALLEY – a place in America where people in nylon stockings make computers.

So I just happened to be mooching about, minding my own business in the kitchen, when Mum came through like a DOUBLE-WHOPPER Lycra-clad express train.

'Hi, Mum,' I said in my 'cute, just hanging about' voice. 'Nice outfit . . . haven't seen that since we were in London.'

'Well, Holly, you've got to live the dream,' Mum said in a 'new' voice I'd never heard before.

'EXCUSE YOU?'

'Well, if I'm going to launch the Hopkinson Farm Emporium, I've got to look the part. It's all part of my PR strategy.'

'Funny you should mention that . . . can I have a word on that front? You see . . .'

So I SPIT-SPOT got my

MAGIC POCKET WATCH out –

THERE WAS NO TIME TO LOSE.

'Mum . . . look very carefully at my **MAGIC POCKET WATCH**.'

'WHERE DID YOU GET THAT, HOLLY?'

'Don't worry about that, Mum . . . just watch it go backwards and forwards, forwards and backwards,' I said calmly and then repeated three verses of **SPIRO, SPERO**.

Mum went nicely

GOGGLE-EYED.

'Mum . . . as ever . . . you will forget you have ever seen my **MAGIC POCKET WATCH**.'

'YES, HOLLY.'

'Now I want to talk to you about what you're going to sell in your farm thingy . . . or rather what you are NOT going to sell.'

'YES, HOLLY.'

'So you are not going to sell scented cushions or naff candles . . . otherwise Harold, Harmony and I will be rounded up by the local kids and evaporated.'

'I UNDERSTAND, HOLLY.'

'Your farm shop cannot be like Mrs Chichester's shop.'

'It's not a shop . . . it's an EMPORIUM.' Mum said defiantly. Which made me realise that my **MAGIC POCKET WATCH** and I had not spelled that bit out.

'Mum . . . you will call it a FARM SHOP and not a FARM EMPORIUM.' I instructed in my 'firm but fair' voice.

'I WILL NOT,'

Mum replied in her 'foot-stamping' voice.

Well, I was shocked – absolutely shocked. I have NEVER had someone bluntly disobey my **MAGIC POCKET WATCH** before.

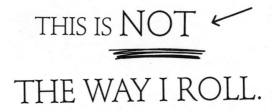

THIS IS NOT

THE WAY I ROLL.

In a panic I decided to shoot a different breeze and did what Mum used to do when she was a PR guru – change the flipping record.

'Mum . . . if you need any FARM SHOP-style live music, The Cool will be your first port to call,' I gabbled.

'Yes, Holly . . . of course,' she replied meekly.

SO HOLLY HOPKINSON IS NOW VERY DOUBLE-WHOPPER SPIT-SPOT CONFUSED ABOUT MUM'S 'PONY WON'T LOAD'* BEHAVIOUR –

WHAT THE HECK

HAPPENED THERE?

---

* **PONY WON'T LOAD** – disobedient, stubborn behaviour.

CHAPTER 16

CONSULTATION WITH AUNT ELECTRA

MUM'S REBELLION AGAINST MY MAGIC POCKET WATCH HAS PUT ME RIGHT OFF MY FOOD – THIS COULD BE THE SLITHERY SLOPE INTO MASS RIOTS AND UNCIVIL UNREST IF I DON'T SORT OUT WHAT'S GONE WRONG HERE. SO I SPIT-SPOT BEETLED ROUND TO THE CHEQUERS TO CONSULT AUNT ELECTRA.

She and Dad were sampling some Smalahove from Norway.

'That sounds nice,' I said. 'What is it, SIL VOU PLATE?'

'It's sheep,' Dad said. So I tasted some.

'Which bit, Dad?' I asked in my 'I'm your youngest daughter and you don't fool me' voice.

'ER . . . WELL . . . IT'S SORT OF SMOKED SHEEP'S HEAD.'

'AND IT IS DEE-LICIOUS,'

Aunt Electra added enthusiastically.

'EXCUSE YOU, are you trying to wipe out the entire population of Lower Goring?' I asked with my hands firmly on my hips. Dad was already bunking off to the bogs after his portion had apparently disagreed with him – he really does have a very weak stomach for a celebrity chef, but at least I had Aunt Electra to myself.

'We have a **PROBLEMO.**' I informed her in my 'secret service' voice. 'Mum has gone rogue.'

Aunt Electra gave a chuckle and rolled her eyes all the way round the back of her head and back.

'Don't we just,' she nodded. 'Pray tell me more.'

So I gave Aunt Electra the full **DOUBLE-WHOPPER DISASTER** debrief, and all she did was flipping well shake her head as if she was Moggy throwing up a mouse on the carpet in front of the fire.

'Don't you see, Holly? The **MAGIC POCKET WATCH** can see that it's good to stop Mum selling Mrs Chichester-esque tat, but not good to stop her calling the shop an **EMPORIUM** . . . and we'll never know why. It's a force of the universe.'

So **THE MAGIC POCKET WATCH NEWS** is that the universe has some very weird forces – how the heck am I going to explain that to Harold and Harmony? They'll think I'm an **ALIEN** who's just landed, not minding my own business.

CHAPTER 17

VINCE ANNOUNCES *HIS* PLANS

I AM A **MEMOIR** CHRONICLER, A **BAND MANAGER**, A SOMETIME **FILM LOCATION** AND PLACES FINDER AND A **SURVIVALIST** SO I AM NOT GOING TO GET SUCKED INTO MUM'S FARM SHOP. BEFORE I KNOW WHAT'S HAPPENED, I'LL BE STACKING SHELVES AND CHANGING THE SELL-BY DATES ON YOGHURTS (WHICH WON'T BE THE FIRST TIME MY FAMILY AND FRIENDS HAVE SUCKED ME INTO A **LIFE OF CRIME**).

I DO need to be firm about this – because I think you'll find that Samuel Pepys didn't do a shift every day lining the labels of the organic BAKED BEANS up before he got his quill and ink out – so neither will Holly Hopkinson.

I am, OF COURSE, also Grandpa's racing manager, and it was in that capacity that I mooched over to Vince's farm to see Le Prince and Declan. I was naturally expecting Vinnie to be there doing jockey stuff – but you will NEVER guess who else was there?!!

DAFFODIL AND FELICITY SNOOP – looking at ~~Grandpa's~~ my racehorses, THANK you very much. And Vinnie was showing off to them and bigging himself up just to batter the bit of cod that was slapping me round my chops.

'All riight?' said Vinnie, going bright red like he'd just been caught red-handed with his hand in a pot of paint.

'OH!' I said in my 'pretend surprise' voice. 'Wasn't expecting to see you guys here.'

'OH, HI, HOLLY,'

Daffodil replied in her 'nervous' voice.

Felicity Snoop didn't say anything so I was NOT going to grovel to her with pheasantries* such as,

'HOW DO YOU DO?'

'Good to see Declan's settling down,' Daffodil observed.

Daffodil is a lot keener on riding (6/10) than I am (0/10), but I knew she was just keeping the conversation away from:

1. Best-friend status.

2. Bossy Bossom's bridesmaids' list.

3. Felicity Snoop leaning over the gate that Grandpa and I lean over to watch Le Prince and Declan.

* PHEASANTRIES – pretty words flying about.

And then guess who wanders up, chewing grass, without a care in the world?

YES.

Vinnie's uncle, Vince.

''Ow's 'Olly?' Vince asked in his 'chatty' voice.

'Good, thanks . . . 'ow are the horses?' I replied in 'Vince' speak.

'GRAND.'

Then Vince spat out *HIS NEWS.*

''Ave you 'eard? We's doin' a festival,' Vince announced proudly, tipping his cap on to the back of his head like he's some duke.

I was deafeningly silent as Lower Goring's hungriest farmer laid out his plans for his music EXTRAVAGANZA. And as reported in the village hall, you get free entry if you bring an animal with you.

'Which is why 'e's callin' it BEASTIVAL.' Vince finished.

(When I told Dad, he said Las Vegas might as well shut up shop.)

Vince is one crafty farmer – I just hope he doesn't think this is going to be a source of food for:

1. Dad's new menu.

2. Mum's farm shop.

Because some people are like that – they will eat virtually anything that comes their way.

CHAPTER 18

BACK AT THE RANCH

THERE WAS A DISTINCT DEEP-FREEZE
ATMOSPHERE WHEN I GOT BACK TO
THE FARM-SHOP LOCATION. AND I CAN SEE
DOUBLE-WHOPPER TROUBLE
WITH A CAPITAL T COMING DOWN THE LINE
LIKE A BULL WITH ITS BOTTOM ON
FIRE IN A CHINA SHOP.

So this is what happened. Mum was in the farmyard, making her architect's head hurt over the plans for her SHOP, when The Cool decided to have a run-through of one of their new songs that Shovel brought with him. Apparently it was tremendously noisy, and Mum stormed into the recording shed like a teacup and told them to cut it out.

Well, that is NOT how showbiz works. So, as **THE COOL** band manager, I'm going to have to tell Mum she is slap bang out of order – I just wish I'd chucked some recording-shed clause into my last **MAGIC POCKET WATCH** chat with her.

> **BAD NEWS** – Harmony and Harold are giving ME a flipping hard time for failing to get Mum to drop the emporium name.

MORE BAD NEWS – the Smalahove has officially made its way all through my body. I need to continue to expand my horizons but it seems my stomach isn't cut out for all this worldly new food either – there will be trouble if anyone nicks the roll of loo paper that I have had to put in the fridge. I shall be recommending this Norwegian delicacy to Harold and Harmony.

A **DARK** CLOUD IS HANGING OVER MY SURVIVALIST PLANS – I NEED TO GET OUT OF THIS PLACE AND HAVE SOME PERSONAL TIME WITH ALEESHAA. PERHAPS SHE CAN INTRODUCE ME TO HER THERAPIST?

CHAPTER 19

THE GRANDPA INQUISITION

AFTER A **SLEEPLESS** NIGHT, I AM NOT IN THE BEST OF HUMOURS. IN FACT, I DON'T KNOW HOW ANYONE GETS A **WINK OF SLEEP** IN THE COUNTRYSIDE. IT'S LIKE TRYING TO KIP IN AN **ALL-NIGHT ANIMAL DISCO.**

First the mice in the attic had a Scottish-dancing marathon, wearing clogs – they might even have had a set of bagpipes with them for all I know – and then a couple of owls had a barney in the garden.

But the worst was when a muntjac kicked off – I have never heard a racket like it. Screeching its head off like crazy. Vinnie says it's a mating call – well, good luck with that. I don't expect any EXPRESSO dating agency to be recommending anything similar for human beings. The council would never put up with that in London.

NEVER.

Then the creaky footsteps and pipe-banging noises started in the attic again – so I started making some snoring noises in case it was Mabel.

GIVE ME A CAR ALARM GOING OFF ALL NIGHT ANY TIME.

At least THAT has a soothing lullaby effect when you're trying to get some kip.

So I was not at my brightest for my job today. Which is to get Grandpa on his own – particularly well away from Vera, who will be doing her usual spy-hovering – and get to the bottom of his secret-family situation.

Grandpa had his noggin in the middle of the *Racing Post* when I crept up to him in an 'innocent' sort of way.

'Look at my **MAGIC POCKET WATCH**, Grandpa,' I commanded. 'Backwards and forwards, forwards and backwards.'

It was quite a job to get him away from the runners at Cheltenham that afternoon, so I gave him four verses of **SPIRO, SPERO** – rather a strong dose for anyone.

He looked well and truly cooked by the fourth verse.

'Grandpa . . . I need to have a little chat with you . . . nothing to worry about.'

'Yes, Holly . . . Is it about Declan . . . or Le Prince?'

'No . . . not really . . . You see . . . I was wondering . . . well . . . do you have a secret family . . . with secret grandchildren . . . that you haven't told us about?'

'WHAT ARE YOU TALKING ABOUT?'

'Are we going to have to leave the farm to make way for them?'

'HOLLY ... HAVE YOU GONE MAD?
WHAT'S THIS ALL ABOUT?'

'What about Vera ... is there anything you need to tell me about her? Because, if Vinnie is some sort of step-cousin, I WILL need therapy.'

'Has someone been telling you stories ... ? Absolutely NOT,' Grandpa replied in his 'this is nonsense' voice.

So I took a deep breath and took the plunge – face first.

'Grandpa, you know you have those pictures in the attic ... ?'

'Good Lord ... I'd forgotten about THEM.'

'Well, why are they up there? Did some other grandchildren you haven't told us about do them? You can be honest with me, Grandpa . . . I won't be cross . . . you WILL be honest with me.'

'Absolutely not . . . . I did them a very long time ago . . . Haven't the mice eaten them by now?'

Well, you could have DOUBLE-WHOPPER blown me off my chair at fifty paces with the Charge of the Light Brigade.

'EXCUSE YOU . . .
YOU DID THEM?'

'They're rubbish . . . I should have thrown them away years ago.'

'But you're a farmer, Grandpa . . . farmers don't do pictures . . . they drive tractors and eat things . . . they don't have time for messing around with paint . . . anyway, they'd get cow doings all over everything.'

'I wasn't always a farmer, you know. Once upon a time, I lived in New York with your grandma and your aunt, and that's when these pictures were painted . . . as I said, a very long time ago . . . should have just left them there.'

Then it all started coming back to me – Aunt Electra hadn't been joking me when she'd been telling me stuff about New York after all*.

'But, Grandpa, did you paint real pictures as well as paint shapes?'

Grandpa chuckled and scratched his forehead.

'You're right . . . that's all they are . . . it was all nonsense . . . but Grandma made me bring them home from New York with us, and I promised her that I'd never throw them away.'

'So Aunt Electra WAS in New York with you?' I asked in my 'detective' voice.

'Yes . . . she quite liked it actually . . . unlike your father . . . his chest couldn't take the air . . . so we had to send him home.'

* If this is confusing then you need to read *A little bit of a BIG disaster!*

> ## 'HE HATED IT?'

'Oh yes . . . the city that never sleeps did not suit your dad.'

> ## 'WHY NOT?'

'Because he couldn't sleep. New York is SO noisy . . . and the food is full of sugar . . . even the bread . . . especially the bread actually . . . maybe that's what inspires his mad food ideas now . . . all that rubbish he had to eat in New York . . . and it made him cough . . . luckily for him, or your grandmother would never have sent him home!'

CATERING NEWS – interesting that Grandpa let slip that he thinks Dad's menus are BONKERS.

PS I AM QUITE RELIEVED THAT VINNIE IS NOT MY COUSIN – don't get me wrong, I like Vinnie, but I do not want to be genetically handcuffed to him.

PPS I am very relieved that we don't have artist cousins who are about to evict us – my hopes of survival have just improved a bit.

SECRET NEWS – I have found out from my mum that a high-security subcommittee of the VCEOC met under a shawl of secrecy – excluding certain biscuit-throwing troublemakers – to discuss some of the finer details of this year's Lower Goring's Got Talent.

Three things to report:

1. They all skewwhiff fell out with each other over where Lower Goring's Got Talent is going to be held. Mum wanted to stage it in what she is still calling her farm EMPORIUM. Mrs Smartside was pulling rank and saying it had to be in the village hall, and then Aunt Electra threw her oar into the drum and said it should be at the Chequers.

2. Mum told Dad that Mrs Chichester is 'such a . . .' because she tipped the vote in favour of the village hall for Mrs Smartside. (Given that my memoirs will be in libraries and museums, I'm not going to write the word Mum used – pardon her French – but it's a farmyard animal and it rhymes with now.)

3. Vince has insisted that all the acts in Lower Goring's Got Talent will have to have 'animal representation' if they want to win the GOLDEN TICKET to play at Beastival because taking an animal to his music festival is its main theme.

CHAPTER 20
BIG LONDON NEWS

MISS BOSSOM WAS LIKE A CAT ON A
HOT TIN ESCALATOR WHEN
WE GOT TO SCHOOL SO I KNEW
SOMETHING WAS UP.

'I have exciting NEWS,' she announced, clapping her hands loudly. 'We're all going to London to visit some art galleries to broaden your horizons.'

What going to London has to do with the sky meeting the earth makes no sense at all and probably explains why Miss Bossom doesn't teach geog.

'Will we be going to the Royal Academy?' asked Felicity Snoop in her 'know-all' voice.

'YES, INDEED, FELICITY.'

'My parents know the director . . . I've already been once.'

'Yes . . . well, it will be a bit of an ADVENTURE for the others, Felicity. Not everyone is as up on their art as you, dear.'

'Will the queen be there?' asked Daffodil, ever hopeful of joining the queue of waiting ladies.

'NO, DEAR . . . SHE'S TOO BUSY.'

Vinnie did not look like any of this **NEWS** was glad tidings – it wouldn't surprise me if he goes spit-spot vamoose come the day of our trip. He'll probably be struck down by some rare animal **DISEASE** that only lasts twenty-four hours.

But it is all **VERY GOOD NEWS** for Holly Hopkinson.

I can smell a bit of London fresh air at the end of the tunnel as the great city awaits the return of a long-lost daughter. I need to use this trip to regain the mortal high ground in my class.

MY OFFICIAL PLAN.

It will not have escaped your attention that ALEESHAA, my town best friend, has a dad who owns an art gallery in Notting Hill, London. So dropping in there will BIG me up MASSIVELY in front of Daffodil.

AND, if I PR up Miss Bossom, it will also be an opportunity to show Aleeshaa that I'm cool and connected, and not just a codswallop Chipping-Topley-area person,

thank you

VERY

much.

HI, ALEESHAA, EVERYTHING COOL MY END – I HAVE A BIG-SHOT RECLUSIVE ART COLLECTOR CLIENT AND SHE MIGHT LIKE TO BUY SOME PICTURES. SHALL I BRING HER TO YOUR DAD'S GALLERY? HOLLY X

PS HOPE YOUR THERAPY IS GOING WELL & WOT IS GALLERY CALLED?

HEY, HOL – RANDOM – MY DAD HAS LOADS OF GOOD STUFF – BRING HER SOON – IT'S SELLING FAST. GALLERY CALLED BLACK HEBESPHENOMEGACORONA

COOL – MY BIG-SHOT RECLUSIVE COLLECTOR LIKES TO BE INCLOGNITO* AND DISGUISE HERSELF BY PRETENDING SHE'S A SCHOOLTEACHER – SO SHE'LL BRING A LOAD OF KIDS WITH HER. THINK YOUR SPELLCHECK GONE BONKERS – WOT NAME OF GALLERY AGAIN?

Aleeshaa texted the gallery name again – it IS called Black Hebesphenomegacorona. I looked it up:

HEBESPHENOMEGACORONA *n.* a polyhedron, a solid figure with flat faces, specifically an irregular one with twenty-one faces, eighteen of them triangular and the other three square.

* INCLOGNITO – wearing weird outfits and shoes.

Aleeshaa's dad must be what Dad calls 'very pretend-tious', if you ask me.

What a DOOFUS.

But I think Daffodil will be DOUBLE-WHOPPER impressed that I hang out in places like this when I'm in Notting Hill. So I'm expecting to be the bee's knees in the Lower Goring pecking order after this expedition!!

CHAPTER 21

HAS LOWER GORING ACTUALLY GOT TALENT?

MRS SMARTSIDE WAS RIGHT ABOUT THE PRESS INTEREST IN LOWER GORING'S GOT TALENT. MY NEW FRIEND FROM THE *DAILY CHIPPING TOPLEY MAIL* AND THE WOMAN FROM ROUNDABOUTCHIPPINGTOPLEY.COM BOTH TURNED UP – BUT NO TELEVISION CAMERAS.

Mum and Aunt Electra were DOUBLE-WHOPPER Guy Fawkes scale NOT HAPPY about failing to secure the location rights for the talent show, and I think they quietly encouraged Harmony to demonstrate* outside the village hall.

But things didn't work out for Harmony on two fronts plus one.

* DEMONSTRATE – to shout and scream like the devil.

1. Slight damp drizzle falling, which, quite frankly, is not ideal if you're standing around, protesting.

2. Harmony prefers it when there are TV cameras present – and she'd done her make-up and everything.

3. The town mob from the new Olde Worlde houses were there, protesting against Beastival noise nuisance.

So Harmony found herself on the same protesting side as the town mob, who don't want pop groups such as The Cool making a noise – and EVEN Harmony could work out that was the flipping wrong side of right to be on.

As you know, Dad says Harmony is growing up fast – which is probably why she threw her placard over the hedge and paid her £1 to come into the village hall and watch the competition.

IT'S

SHOW TIME!

The official judging panel was Mrs Smartside (automatic* chairperson), Mrs Chichester, Mum and the vicar. Vince then kicked up a big fuss and said he'd take his GOLDEN TICKET home if he wasn't on the judging panel – and Mrs Smartside didn't dare stand her ground because she doesn't want any more out-of-control stories written by you-know-who in the *Daily Chipping Topley Mail.*

They all had a board on which they had to write their score for each act – so there was no way there could be any skewwhiff slippery stuff going on. And guess who got to write the scores down on the OFFICIAL blackboard?

YES.

Holly Hopkinson, thank you very much – and I should think so too after all the sweeping up I had to do after the biscuit fight. (I think it's also a sign that I'm going to be offered a position on the general committee fairly soon.)

---

* AUTOMATIC – immediately assumes control.

I did think about declaring 'my interest'. But me and my **MAGIC POCKET WATCH** are perfectly capable of managing **THE COOL** and not corrupting a scoreboard, thank you very MUCH – after all,

I can't **HYPNOTISE** a whole

flipping

village hall full of people.

There were six acts – and Mrs Smartside randomly pulled their order of appearance out of one of the late Mr Smartside's hats.

'I declare the first act will be . . . Daffodil Chichester and *Swan Lake*,' she declared.

The lights in the hall were switched off, and a spotlight lit up the stage – and then Daffodil rushed on to it with a scented cushion under her arm in the shape of a swan.

She looked as keen as custard. With big white wings, she swooped around, like FAIRIES do, to some violin music that wasn't bad at all. Daffodil IS a **DARK HORSE**, as I have noted before – I had no idea she could write music like that.

At the end, I cheered madly for Daffodil (even though I want The Cool to win), and Mrs Smartside got to her feet like a sea lion does when it decides to go for a swim.

'Ladies and gentlemen . . . another round of applause for Daffodil Chichester and *Swan Lake*. We shall vote from my right to left. Judges . . . are you ready?'

They all started scribbling, looking dead-whopper serious, and then nodded.

First up was Mrs Chichester. She held her board in front of her as if she was showing off one of her cushions.

 'TEN,'

announced Mrs Smartside in her 'pleased' voice.

Then it was the vicar's turn to display his score. He held it up as if it was one of the Ten Commandments.

'FOUR,'

Mrs Smartside said in her 'less pleased' voice. 'My turn now . . . Ten.'

Mum and Vince exchanged **CONSPIRATORIAL** secret glances and started to rub out the numbers they'd originally written on their boards.

 shouted Mrs Chichester at Mrs Smartside. 'They're changing their scores.'

'NO RULE 'GAINST THAT,'

barked Vince.

'SALLY?' enquired Mrs Smartside in her 'suspicious' voice.

Mum looked like someone in a film who was about to do something DOUBLE-WHOPPER dodgy – and then she held her board up.

– NUL POINTS,

as they say in Papua New Guinea.

Then, Bob's your uncle, the village hall went flipping bonkers – there was hooting and banging. I have NEVER heard such a din.

And you WILL NOT believe what happened next.

YES.

Vince held his board up, and it said zero too.

Mrs Chichester started shouting stuff, and Vince shouted back. Mum looked like she was trying to be invisible, and Mrs Smartside looked like a cheese soufflé bursting out of its dish.

137

Obviously, with my Holly Hopkinson (band manager's) hat on, I was quite pleased that Mum and Vince kept Daffodil's score down to twenty-four.

But Holly Hopkinson (schoolgirl) thought their scores were a bit stingy.

Finally the **MADDENING** crowd was stilled for Act Two – which was Vinnie. Vera was very dramatic as she announced his act.

'For the first time ever in the Chipping Topley area, Vinnie will perform a still-life demonstration of Domino, his VENTRILOQUIST snail . . . This requires absolute quiet from the audience because Domino is very shy and won't say anything if you scare him.'

She wasn't kidding. I think the whole rumpus that erupted after the Daffodil voting shenanigans put that snail right off his stride. He never said a word.

After what seemed like an **ETERNITY.** Mrs Smartside said, 'Time's up,' and the judges wrote down their scores.

'Right,' said Mrs Smartside in her 'high sheriff' voice. 'WE shall start the voting from the other end this time. Anyone in the audience who shouts out will be ejected.'

Mum gave Vinnie nine out of ten, and Vince voted ten! There were a lot of **NOISES** in the hall, but not technically shouting out. More like farmyard noises.

Then it was the vicar's turn. He went for a safe five. He knows which side his congregation butter their bread!

Mrs Smartside held up a defiant

ZERO,

and Mrs Chichester followed suit, as they say in smart London clubs.

That left Vinnie on twenty-four points – in a play-off with Daffodil.

Next up was Miss Bossom. Slinky Dave was in charge of lighting and music on the stage. He looked like Andrew Lord Webber at the *School of Rock* production with his headphones on, twiddling knobs and stuff.

It was quite a performance.

Bossy dashed round the stage, looking dramatic, with veils going everywhere – she nearly tripped over one of them. And she must have been flipping hot because, by the end of her dance, she'd got rid of seven of them.

If I'm honest, it's not what you want to see your teachers getting up to in their free time. But the audience loved it. They were cheering and clapping, and Bossy bigged herself up afterwards, bowing and scraping on her knees.

Mrs Smartside changed the voting order again and let herself go first as she was in the middle. She clearly did not like Botty's carry-on – and only gave her a one. The audience booed like a herd of

BISON.

The vicar was next – and you could have blown me down with a bucket of rusty veils. He gave her

TEN.

Mum voted five, so – surprise, surprise – Mrs Chichester voted six just to get one over on her with Miss Bossom, thank you

very much.

Finally Vince voted three – which he thought was a low score – but Vince isn't famous for his counting skills unless it's how many steaks he's got on his plate – and his vote meant that Bossy Bossom had collected twenty-five points and was in the lead – the DOOFUS!

Sir Garfield, Dad's cricketing butcher friend, was the next act.

'Gary will entice his ferret to enter one trouser leg by the shoe department and leave his trousers via the alternative shoe,' his manager officially announced. (Don't ask me why Dad calls him Gary – it's probably a nickname.)

The 'act' had its moments, but probably not for the main stage at Beastival.

Sir Garfield amassed a grand DOUBLE-WHOPPING total of seventeen votes.

As predicted, the competition had drawn acts in from far and wide hoping to win the GOLDEN TICKET. and a boy band from Harold's school at Chipping Topley called Marshmallow and Cream turned up.

But the **BAD NEWS** was, as far as Holly Hopkinson (The Cool's band manager) was concerned, that Marshmallow and Cream were really good.

If I hadn't been on scoring duty, I'd have given them three verses of sPiRo, sPeRo and signed them up.

Vince voted first. He'd been doing his sums and realised he'd knocked his own nephew out, so he clearly wanted this lot instead of Miss Bossom at Beastival. He gave them ten!

Mum was having none of it and gave them

Mrs Smartside did not like being bellowed at 'by young men in silly trainers' so she joined Mum and gave them zero too.

The vicar, who nearly always votes somewhere in the middle, gave them five, but Mrs Chichester, who never votes nicely, and was furious that she HADN'T been bellowed at, gave them zero.

Final total for Marshmallow and Cream = fifteen*.

That just left the GRAND FINALE – and, as Harmony wasn't outside in the drizzle protesting any more, I appointed her The Cool's OFFICIAL announcer – because, a bit like Aunt Electra, Harmony can turn it on when it comes to the amateur-dramatic bigging-things-up bit.

'LADIES AND GENTLEMEN . . . FOR ONE NIGHT ONLY . . . PUT YOUR HANDS TOGETHER FOR THE COOLEST BAND TO EVER COME OUT OF LOWER GORING . . .'

* FIFTEEN – having finished last, Marshmallow and Cream turned out to not be as sweet as they looked or sounded – they kicked the dustbins over on their way out, scattering fragmented biscuits ALL OVER THE PLACE.

Someone in the audience shouted, 'More like the only band to ever come out of Lower Goring!' and everyone started laughing.

Harmony well and truly had the wind taken out of her socks – but pulled it around to announce officially,

'THE COOL!'

Harold was the first on to the stage. Someone had given him a funny black hat that looked like one of Vera's burned pork pies, and he had a black T-shirt and black jeans on – so don't blame me if he gets flipping well run over while he's walking back to the farm.

Stickly was next – waving to the audience in a cool way and looking like he was half asleep.

And then in his own time – after an unnecessary pause, thank you very much – Shovel ambled on to the stage like he thinks HE'S the star of the show.

Shovel needs to do something about his personal hyena and go and visit the hair cutter's. There was a right whiff that nearly knocked me double-whopper flying when he came past – he will be getting six verses of **SPIRO, SPERO** from my **MAGIC POCKET WATCH** if he doesn't have a bath anytime soon! (Although, as will become apparent, it was important that my **MAGIC POCKET WATCH** didn't enforce that cleanliness before this evening.)

But THERE IS a problem with The Cool – and this is me, Holly Hopkinson (their manager), admitting it! Harold has found his mojo and is no longer terrified. And he's pretty good at hitting the drums; Stickly is excellent at doing stretches, looking **COOL** and twanging his guitar a bit. So far so good.

Then they all start to sing at the same time; but as far as I can make out they don't all sing the same song. Well, that's what it sounds like.

Thank goodness they were only allowed to sing different songs at the same time for one song, if you get my drift.

'Thank you for that noise,' Mrs Smartside said in her 'poshest' voice while looking down her nose as if she'd stepped in a pile of horse doings.

'Charmian, why don't you vote first?' she requested with the addition of a furtive, fake smile.

'I'D BE DELIGHTED TO,'

Mrs Chichester barked, flashing her **FANGS** like a rabid dog.

'ZERO!'

'Vicar . . . your go,' Mrs Smartside ordered.

The vicar voted true to form – in the middle. 'Five.'

A flicker of alarm flashed across Mrs Smartside's severe-looking eyebrows as she did a few mental calculations.

'My vote . . . terrible racket,' Mrs Smartside declared. 'Zero.'

Mrs Chichester, who doesn't have calculus embroidery on her candles, gave a smug snigger.

 **'TEN,'** Mum then hissed defiantly.

Mrs Smartside let out a noise that is probably illegal in some parts of the world.

So it was down to Vince the Kingmaker. Ten points would put The Cool in a tie; anything less would leave Miss Bossom the outright winner.

Mrs Chichester's finger calculations had finally caught up, and she was no longer sniggering.

Vince cleared his throat in a farmer-ish sort of way.

'My vote . . . TEN,' he said, as if he was scolding one of his sheepdogs. 'But that's not all,' he added. 'I got objection to Miss Bossom's act.'

Mrs Smartside was now boiling like cabbage, and she'd long forgotten that she'd only given Bossy one point.

'ON WHAT GROUNDS?'

she bellowed.

'NO ANIMALS REPRESENTED IN 'ER PERFORMANCE,'

Vince replied.

Then Mrs Chichester put her hand up, just like Felicity Snoop does in class, as she blathered, 'THE COOL didn't have animal representation either.'

When The Cool write their memoirs and look back on their long and successful careers, I'm sure they will reflect on how their manager was on top of things the night they got their big break.

Because Holly Hopkinson (Band Manager Inc.) had thought this one through and, just to play safe, had informed Vince before the competition had started why THE COOL would be compliant, as they say in the music business, with the rules of the competition.

'Oh yes, they did,' Vince said in his 'I know me onions' voice. 'Cos Shovel's got lice . . . that'll do fer me.'

Well, there was a right carry-on after Vince dropped that bombshell – and I think it's best for the adults if I leave my coverage of Lower Goring's Got Talent here, because none of them come out of what happened next well.

I will just say that Miss Bossom's claim to have nits failed, as far as Vince was concerned, because nits are only eggs, and he clearly stated 'animals'.

BUT THESE ARE MEANT TO BE DOUBLE-WHOPPER SERIOUS MEMOIRS, AND THAT IS ALL I AM PREPARED TO CHRONICLE ON THIS MATTER.

CHAPTER 22

LONDON'S CALLING

I MANAGED TO GET BOTTY BOSSOM ON HER OWN THIS MORNING AS SHE WAS COMING OUT OF THE STAFFROOM WITH HER PONGING-COFFEE STINKY BREATH.

'Miss Bossom, please would you look at my MAGIC POCKET WATCH?'

'How nice, Holly . . . where did you get that?'

'You see, it goes backwards and forwards, forwards and backwards,' I replied, not getting distracted by her chitchat.

And then I gave her three verses of SPIRO, SPERO – nice and slowly – and she looked as cooked as a cooked thing on National Cooked Day by the time I'd finished.

'Miss Bossom . . . you are going to take our class to Aleeshaa's dad's art gallery in Notting Hill today, and you are going to pretend that you are a big-shot reclusive art collector.'

'YES, HOLLY . . . BUT WILL THEY BELIEVE THAT?'

'Oh yes . . . don't worry about that,' I told Miss Bossom in my 'reassuring' voice.

So I think it's pretty clear that it's going to be *good* and *fun* for Miss Bossom to look like a big shot in Aleeshaa's dad's gallery.

Slinky Dave had the bus all polished up, and he put on quite a show for Miss Bossom driving to London; he was covered in aftershave – the whole bus whiffed of it, thank you very much!

As predicted, no sign of Vinnie for this Tour de Culture – the official excuse was that he had a desperate dose of the trots and was unable to venture far from his facilities. More like he's taken Le Prince out for a trot, but it's not for me to blow the gasket off Vinnie's lie-abi*.

Miss Bossom officially announced the plan for the day as we hurtled down the motorway past the 'rotten service' station.

ART NEWS –

on our LONDON trip we are going to the Royal Academy first – where no doubt the director will be on hand to big up Felicity Snoop – and then we're going to walk to the National Gallery because Slinky Dave says parking is a nightmare. So it's obviously a pretty rubbish place if they don't even have their own car park – even the Chipping Topley library's got one.

'And then, children, a special surprise,' Botty Bossom declared. 'Holly Hopkinson has arranged for us to visit the famous Black Hebesphenomegacorona gallery.'

---

* LIE-ABI – untruthful excuse.

Well, you should have seen Felicity Snoop's face! Just as she thought she was going to be the clever-clogs big cheese of the art trip, I stuck a double-whopper bogey right back up her nose – although I hadn't been expecting Miss Bossom to blow my own trumpet for me with the 'surprise visit' announcement.

Daffodil was so excited when she got off the bus at the Royal Academy she was exploding like corn in a POPCORN popper. Thank goodness she had a hat on – otherwise her brains might have blasted all over the place.

The poor girl is under the impression that this is a school for royal children (for some reason lost on me), and she thinks she's going to meet some of them.

DAFFODIL IS **DESPERATE** TO BECOME ONE OF THOSE WOMEN WHO SIT AROUND ALL DAY WAITING AND KNITTING IN CASE THE QUEEN WANTS SOMEONE TO PLAY WITH.

Sure enough, someone with a clipboard was 'on standby' for the arrival of 'Felicity Snoop and her class'. Daffodil stuck to her like glue, full of expectation – knees bent and courtesies at the ready. But there wasn't a royal nipper anywhere in sight – they'd probably all gone to play polo for the day. And I can't say I blame them for two reasons and probably more.

1. There were rubberneckers like Daffodil all over the place – how any school is meant to function when it's full of people gawping, I do not know.

2. Somebody had let a bunch of kids stick a load of rubbish up on the walls.

You've never seen anything like it. It was chaos; a shambles; a total fiasco; utter **BEDLAM**; complete PANDEMONIUM; skewwhiff spanner-in-the-works disarray, to put it mildly!

Half of the pictures weren't even finished: arms missing, even heads. Some didn't have frames. Even making allowances for the fact that most of the kids are probably in nursery school, it was

embarrassing.

Next stop was the National Gallery in Trafalgar Square. And I have to say this is MORE LIKE it, even if it hasn't got a flipping car park.

---

1. From a PR point of view, as Mum would say, first impressions are very important, and they have done a great job cleaning up the square since the battle – the building looks terrific. You just wouldn't know they'd been firing cannons all over the place.

2. The café is spit-spot.

3. Every picture is finished.

4. They all have very nice gold frames, and you just can't beat that.

And the great thing about the National Gallery is that there's something for everyone: pictures of fields, mountains, seas or just people. OK, some of the older folk in the paintings are way out of shape and really need to get a grip; they HAVE NOT been squeezing ANY value out of their gym memberships; and some of them might like to think about covering up a bit.

'THAT'S ENOUGH, BOYS ... KEEP MOVING ... AND NO POINTING, GASPAR.'

a huffing Miss Bossy Bossom said in her 'agitated' voice, and then went bright red like she'd done one.

This was a big improvement on the first place.

CHAPTER 23

ADVANCE TO NOTTING HILL

SLINKY DAVE HAD THE BUS'S ENGINE
REVVING FOR US WHEN WE CAME BACK
OUT ON TO THE OLD BATTLEGROUND –
ALL READY TO HEAD UP TO THE BLACK
HEBESPHENOMEGACORONA GALLERY.

This is going to be my DOUBLE-WHOPPER Holly
Hopkinson is a hip-hop arty London chic moment
that my classmates will never forget. And I'll look
cool in front of Aleeshaa.

ON OUR WAY

I texted to Aleeshaa.

RANDOM –
SEE YA IN THE HOOD

Aleeshaa replied.

I don't get this random nonsense – and something was making me feel very unrelaxed.

'Well, Holly – we are looking forward to this,' Miss Bossom said in a 'strange' voice.

As she got off the bus, there was this DRAMATIC transformation. Bossy put on a big Burberry overcoat, with her collar turned up, and a pair of dark glasses and, blow me down with a Trafalgar cannon, Slinky Dave did the same; except he had a long dark overcoat on.

'EXCUSE YOU . . .
WHAT ARE YOU PLAYING AT?'

I asked Slinky Dave in my 'ABSOLUTELY FURIOUS' voice.

'She's told me I'm her bodyguard . . . just in case there's any trouble.'

Anyway, I needn't have worried about Bossy Bossom and Slinky Dave's outfits – EVERY other person in the gallery was wearing dark glasses. Botty Bossom just looked like all the other reclusive art collectors except she'd brought her large family with her – adopted, of course. That's the way they roll in Notting Hill.

As for it being a gallery, it's no more a gallery than the junk shop that used to be on the corner of our street in London. There were bits and pieces lying around everywhere. I can flipping well see why Aleeshaa calls everything random.

And, speak of the devil, there she was, looking all COOL, hanging out in the corner, huddled up with some boy like they had the BIGGEST SECRET in the world.

'Hello, Aleeshaa . . . good to see you . . . how are you?' I asked in my 'cool' voice as I walked up to them, using my casual 'when in Rome' walk.

'Yeah . . . random . . . this is Dice.'

Dice made a sort of urban grunt and just looked at the floor.

'How do you do, Dice?' I asked in my 'arty-edgy' voice.

'Yeah . . . random,' he replied. It was a pity I didn't have Vinnie with me to shoot the breeze with Dice.

'So where are the pictures?' I asked Aleeshaa, now switching to my 'businesslike' voice.

'PICTURES?'

'Yes . . . pictures. You said your dad had an art gallery.'

'THIS IS, LIKE, ART.'

I cast a snooty glance round the room for effect.

'This is, like, a spare-parts warehouse for second-hand cars, thank you very much,' I said.

If Aleeshaa thought she could petrolise me with her urban attitude, she had another thing coming. But, just as I was about to straighten her out, up came some dude wearing trousers that had shrunk in the wash, no socks and a goat's beard – and then I recognised him – it was Aleeshaa's dad.

'Hey, Holly Hopkinson, look at you! So I hear you've brought a "face" with you? Thank you . . . we'll take good care of you, of course.'

'Hello, Mr Smith,' I said, wondering if that included sandwiches.

'Er . . . it's de Medici,' he replied in his 'whispering' voice.

'EXCUSE YOU?'

'De Medici . . . we've . . . er . . . changed our name to de Medici.'

Well, I had not seen that one coming, thank you very much. And the goat's beard – where had he got that from?

'So the lady over there is your reclusive art collector?' Aleeshaa's dad asked, looking towards Miss Bossom and Slinky Dave.

'Er . . . yes, that's her . . . but she can't stay long. She's got to fly to New York . . . you know how it is. In fact, it's pictures she's after really, not second-hand car engines.'

Mr Smith – or shall we say de Medici in case historians reading this get muddled – moved away from the lump of metal that someone had left in the wrong place on the floor.

'Hmmm . . . pictures . . . New York . . . Expressionists?' he asked, flicking his eyebrows towards his ears.

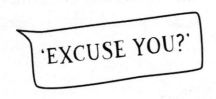

'EXCUSE YOU?'

'Expressionists . . . does she like abstract expressionists . . . New York?'

'Oh yes . . . she loves those,' I said in my 'knowledgeable' voice.

Quicker than you could say Jumping Jack Flash, Mr de Medici was hanging off Miss Bossom's elbow and escorting her through to another room.

On the plus side, there were things hanging on the walls in there. But they weren't real pictures – just flipping shapes and paint all over the place – and not a decent frame in sight, but Bossy Bossom was really playing up to the part.

'Oh yes . . . very . . . very interesting,' she said in her 'slow' voice while she looked at a picture of a load of squares dumped on top of each other – not even stacked properly.

Mr de Medici nodded repeatedly, and for one moment I thought he was going to dribble out of the side of his mouth like Barkley does when he watches the dog-food adverts between races on TV.

Then, as they looked at the pictures, I was stunned as if a **GIANT OCTOPUS** had just hit me over the head with an anvil.

It flipping well jumped off the wall at me – I'd know one of them anywhere. I just stood and gulped at it.

'Now this is a real collector's item,' Mr de Medici whispered perspirationally* into Botty's ear as I swallowed a bit like Barkley does when he eats too fast.

'Enlighten me, Mr de Medici, enlighten me,' purred Miss Bossom.

'We call him the lost artist – one of the great abstract expressionist painters in New York, right up there with Jackson Pollock and Mark Rothko . . . but he just disappeared off the face of the earth with all his paintings. I think this is the only one left in England . . .'

> * PERSPIRATIONALLY – sweating while you have good ideas.

'So what's his name?' I asked Aleeshaa's father in my 'no-nonsense' voice.

'Well, Holly, that's the thing . . . he didn't have an artistic name, just an identity. He signed his work with that squiggle in the bottom left of the painting.'

I took a good hard look at the squiggle and snapped a photo of the picture on my smart mobile phone.

Miss Bossom was well into her role of 'big-shot reclusive', but getting less reclusive and more expressive by the minute.

And her bodyguard was beginning to look like he was going to be 'the trouble'. I think Slinky Dave is the jealous type when he's got BOGGLE EYES.

It was time to spit-spot before the whole DOUBLE-WHOPPER shenanigans unravelled around me like a tin of ravioli.

'Er . . . miss . . . I think it's time . . .' and then I started to make frog noises in my throat. How could I tell a schoolteacher who was pretending to be a big-shot reclusive art collector who was in turn pretending to be a schoolteacher that we needed to get our groove on? All in front of Monsieur de Medici-Smith and any other names he's flipping well picked up.

'Um . . . the pilot says you're going to miss your spot back to the school, I'm afraid, if we don't get going . . . and the bus will get stuck in traffic while we're at it,' I whispered into Bossy's ear. It's called covering both bases!

Aleeshaa was nowhere to be seen – she'd probably gone to make the sandwiches – but we had to spit-spot scarper.

AND IT'S SO MUCH COOLER ←

TO LEAVE AND NOT SAY GOODBYE.

o o o

The journey home from Notting Hill WAS NOT my finest odyssey*, thank you very MUCH. I just had to stick it out in the back of the bus while I got buckets of abuse poured over me from the rest of the class, who had, NOT SURPRISINGLY, been most unimpressed by a second-hand car-parts depot posing as an art gallery.

Daffodil gave me an artistic frozen shoulder and made no attempt whatsoever to bagsie the seat next to me on the bus – which I had kept vacationed for her.

WEIRD NEWS –

Miss Bossom KEPT pretending to be a reclusive art collector all the way back to Lower Goring.

EX-BEST FRIEND NEWS –

so much for Aleeshaa. I've a good mind to block her on my smart mobile phone. I can't think why she was EVER my London best friend.

---

if Aleeshaa's father, Monsieur de Medici-Smith can be a hotshot art-gallery owner and art connivanceur**, then why not Holly Hopkinson? If I can be a band manager, a racehorse manager and sometime film location and places double agent, being an art gallery impresso***, as they say in Finland, should be a doddle.

I HAVE A PLAN.

* ODYSSEY – long and peculiar journey sometimes written about in long and boring books.

** CONNIVANCEUR – expert in things.

*** IMPRESSO – bang-on super-fast producer.

CHAPTER 24

POST OUR TRIP TO THE BLACK HEBESPHENOMEGACORONA GALLERY

AS USUAL, I WAS FIRST ON THE BUS THIS MORNING – BECAUSE NO ONE LIVES MORE REMOTELY THAN I DO FROM LOWER GORING SCHOOL, THANK YOU VERY MUCH!

Immediately I could tell all was double-whopper not well in the land of the school bus.

Slinky Dave was slumped in a funk in his driver's seat with a big BLACK cloud hanging over his head.

'GOOD MORNING, DAVE,' I said.

'There's nothing good about it, I can tell you. She's gone and changed all our wedding plans . . . I don't know what's got into her,' Dave said in his 'we've got a three-hour traffic delay' voice.

I could feel my **MAGIC POCKET WATCH** twitching in its belt. So, rather than try and extract info from the gibleting* wreck formerly known as Slinky Dave, I decided to give him three verses of **SPIRO, SPERO** and get to the bottom of the Bossom problem.

'Look at my **MAGIC POCKET WATCH**, Dave . . . forwards and backwards, backwards and forwards.' And then I repeated

'SPIRO, SPERO, SQUIGGLEOUS SCOTCH, CAST YOUR EYES WHITHER MY WATCH.'

three times.

Slinky Dave was in such a **DISTRESSED** state, I think half a verse might have done him.

'Dave . . . you will tell me exactly what has happened with Miss Bossom and your wedding plans . . . spit-spot . . . or we'll be late for school.'

* GIBLETING – empty chicken.

'Well . . . she came back from London, where for some reason she was pretending to be a modern-art collector . . . and she's been acting all funny since . . . like she really is a modern-art collector . . . and everything's being changed.'

 'Everything?'

'Yeah . . . she's thrown all my furniture into the garden shed, and she's only gone and brought everything from the shed into our front room . . . she's put my broken lawn mower where the TV used to be, and she sat on the floor, telling me to explore the post-industrial consequences of progress. What's that got to do with my broken lawn mower?'

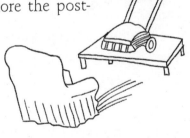

'AND YOUR WEDDING PLANS, DAVE?'

171

'She says, because all the big modern-art collectors will be coming, we have to have an "installation" wedding in a big glass pyramid . . . and we can't have any **EXPLOITATION** of animals*.'

'Well, that's the four black stallions gone then,' I observed. 'And Mrs Chichester's pink doves . . . and no scented cushions or embroidered candles then?' I added in my 'hopeful' voice.

'You're not kidding . . . and guess what? The guest list has completely changed too . . . the invitations will all be colour-coded, and there's going to be an inner sanctum . . .'

'Oh well, I hope I'll be in that,' I said in my 'forgetting myself' voice.

'No way . . . not if you haven't got more than one surname you won't be . . . and all the guests have to come with a rotting turnip on their head to show they're connected to the countryside . . .'

* **EXPLOITATION OF ANIMALS** – Dad says the modern arty lot don't mind skewering butterflies, but they draw the line at letting doves fly around.

'OK, Dave . . . this is really bad. I can see you ARE NOT going to enjoy your wedding one little bit.'

'ENJOY IT? I'M NOT EVEN GOING TO BE THERE!

She says modern-art collectors are so cool they don't even go to their own parties . . . so we're getting married at the registry office and not turning up. You see, she HAS gone bonkers.'

So, as you can tell, Slinky Dave was double-whopper not a happy bunny and it was all my **MAGIC POCKET WATCH's** fault. So Holly Hopkinson (not sure which department) will have to come to the rescue.

○ ○ ○

Things looked worse than I expected when I arrived at school. Miss Bossom was wearing dark glasses and black clothes that were too tight in some places and very baggy in others; and she looked like she'd put her make-up on with her foot.

Then she gave us treble art and banged on all day about stuff we don't know anything about and she knows less. Like cubism, realism, fauvism and minimalism. Which is basically art for people who can't paint normal stuff.

WE HAVE A **PROBLEMO, HOUSTON!**

On the one hand there appear to be many benefits to Mrs Chichester's original wedding plans getting put on a slow boat to nowhere that has been desserted* for decades – and then on to some island full of sand.

But on the other hand Holly Hopkinson and her **MAGIC POCKET WATCH** have got to help Slinky Dave sort his wedding out because that will be *good* for him.

Maybe we can find a solution that suits all parties – except Mrs Chichester, Daffodil and Felicity Snoop . . . and the **LUNATIC** who was going to dye the doves.

* **DESSERTED** – empty place, not to be confused with puddings.

CHAPTER 25
CONSULTATION WITH AUNT ELECTRA

AS SOON AS I GOT BACK TO THE FARM,
I SNIFFED OUT AUNT ELECTRA AND
DEMANDED a TOP-SECRET
OFFICIAL CONFAB.

'Aunt Electra . . . WE have a **SERIOUS** problem,'
I announced in my 'emergency' voice as soon as
we were incommune ocado* in the ARABIAN tent
that was still up in the garden from my birthday
party – leaking quite a lot now.

'We, Holly?' Aunt Electra asked.

'Yes, WE . . . that's you, me and our **MAGIC
POCKET WATCH.**'

---

* INCOMMUNE OCADO – some place no one delivers to.

'I think it's YOUR **MAGIC POCKET WATCH**, my dear, not mine.'

'Excuse you,' I said in my 'furious, absolutely **FURIOUS**' voice. 'If you had made this whole thing a bit simpler, I might not have a rogue teacher going mad! Miss Bossom has got STUCK in modern-art collector mode, thank you VERY much.'

So Aunt Electra came to her senses and we talked about OUR problem. How to return Miss Bossom to being a run-of-the-mill, not very good teacher from Lower Goring.

'Yes . . . this is very unusual,' Aunt Electra admitted. 'I just can't understand it. Maybe it's for good or fun that Miss Bossom still thinks she's a modern-art collector? The **MAGIC POCKET WATCH** normally knows best.'

'Well, it flipping well isn't *good* or *fun* for Slinky Dave . . .'

'But he might find out that a life in Notting Hill drinking **CAPPUCCINOS** with modern-art dealers is more fun than driving a school bus?'

'I don't think so. Dad says they can be tricky tricksters ripping off suckers . . . I do not think Slinky Dave is cut out for that DOUBLE-WHOPPER carry-on.'

'Well, it's most irregular to try and get the **MAGIC POCKET WATCH** to reverse its own work, but I don't reckon it's the first time. I think your Grandma Esme might have resorted to such a thing once in New York so you'll just have to give Miss Bossom three verses of **SPIRO, SPERO** tomorrow and tell her she isn't a modern-art collector.'

'Will that defo work?' I asked in my 'hopeful' voice.

'Well, darling . . . there's only one way to find out,' Aunt Electra drawled in her 'BOHEMIAN' voice.

NOTE TO SELF: when this crisis has passed, I think it's time I learned a bit more about Grandma Esme . . .

CHAPTER 26

BACK TO THE ATTIC

MORNING NEWS

MUM ALREADY HAS BUILDERS CONVERTING THE MAIN BARN INTO THE 'FOOD HALL' SO SHE WAS IN THERE, GIVING THEM SOME VERBAL EXPECTATIONS.

Dad has gone to the Chequers to try out some of his new 'Round the World cuisine'. (Grandpa is calling it Round the Bend cuisine.) He's tasting some Rocky Mountain oysters from America this morning.

'Excuse you . . . I thought oysters came from the sea, not the mountains?' I had pointed out in my 'helpful' voice at breakfast.

'Well, Rocky Mountain oysters are just their nickname . . . They're actually deep-fried bulls' parts.'

Pardon
his French.

You just couldn't make it up – no one eats deep-fried food these days.

Grandpa had his noggin in the *Racing Post*, and I think Barkley's eaten one of his hearing aids, so I didn't need to worry about him.

Then in popped Vinnie, looking very sprightly for a person who only two days ago had been struck down by some form of Vera's **REVENGE.*** preventing him from attending our class's cultural tour of London.

'All riight,' he said in his 'chipper' voice as he waltzed into the kitchen.

'Just the very person I was about to look for,' I replied. 'I need you to accompany me, in the role of assistant, up to the attic.'

* **VERA'S REVENGE** – nasty dose of the runs.

Vinnie pulled a 'pony won't load' face.

'Le Prince felt like a goodun when you were away,' he said in his 'jockey's' voice, which comes out of the side of his mouth.

'Well, I'm glad you could tell that the day before yesterday from the warmth of your bog (that's restroom for my American readers),' I replied.

'ALL RIIGHT,' said Vinnie.

'Anyway, I won't snitch on you, Vinnie, if you give me a secret hand to get into the attic.'

'ALL RIIGHT?'

'We're going to get Grandpa's pictures out of their crates so that I can have a good look at them . . . We might be on to something BIG here, Vinnie.'

'Riight,' was now Vinnie's unenthusiastic response – which in Vinnie language is directly opposite to 'All riight'.

And I began to smell a mouse.

'Vinnie,' I said in my 'kind but harsh' voice, 'did you tell Grandpa that we went up into the attic?'

'Riight,' Vinnie replied elusively.

'Yorkel or shnorkel?'*

Yorkel,' Vinnie admitted, his crestfallen head bowed in disgrace. Yet again, Vinnie has betrayed the Bogey Club.

And then something happened for the first time in history. Grandpa put the *Racing Post* down and shuffled over to talk to me and Vinnie. When the flipping house was burning down, Grandpa hadn't shifted his gaze from his newspaper, so I knew something was up.

'I hear Mabel troubled you the other night, Holly. She hasn't been wandering around for years . . . I wonder what disturbed her?'

'Maybe it was the flipping owl that was running an all-night DISCO outside my bedroom window, Grandpa,' I suggested in my 'diversion tactics innocent youngest granddaughter' voice. 'Perhaps Vince could eat it?'

* SHNORKEL – no in Bogey Club language.

Grandpa gave me a look and then bunked off to 'see a man about a dog', so I think my owl-disinformation tactic worked a treat!

As soon as Grandpa was VANISHO. Vinnie and I sprang spit-spot into action like coiled rings. We were up that ladder with our torches and a chisel that Vinnie had for busting the crates open quicker than you can say greased pole.

So here is a double-whopper OFFICIAL surprise for the world of culture and memoir readers on both sides of the pond moment.

Grandpa was a busy boy when he was in New York – he flipping well had about fifty pictures in the attic, once we'd got them all laid out – and here is the **GOOD NEWS** – double-whopper bingo stop the press and websites for this one. When I got my smart mobile phone out and cranked up the picture in the gallery – guess what?

YES.

THEY ALL HAVE THE FUNNY LITTLE SQUIGGLE THAT MR DE MEDICI-SMITH POINTED OUT TO ME IN THE BOTTOM LEFT-HAND CORNER.

Which means Grandpa is

'THE LOST ARTIST'.

I now knew that I was sitting on the biggest unexploded art bomb that anyone had dug up since the 1950s. Holly Hopkinson is about to become one of the biggest art gallery IMPRESSOS in the world. I just need a good name for my gallery now – and a flipping gallery.

PERSONAL SURGERY NEWS –

this success will not change me. I will not be rushing off to have **BOTOX** injected into my lips, bottom and forehead to make me look surprised for the rest of my life.

I may develop a hard edge to see off the jackals and hyenas – so Aleeshaa is going to officially get the boot.

That is **GOOD NEWS** for Daffodil, who I shall forgive for momentarily abandoning me for Felicity Snoop. I'm sure she will be graceful when it is confirmed that she is resurrected as my official countryside BEST FRIEND.

I shall also be loyal to my friend Vinnie and give him a BIG promotion –

he could be my driver?

Miss Bossom and Vera, on the other hand, may discover the tough side of the art gallery IMPRESSO that is Holly de Hopkinson.

LIGHTBULB MOMENT NEWS –

Holly Hopkinson (Film Location and Places Inc.) has been up all night, pondering picture-display issues – and then, just as the owl was kicking off, it hit me like a double-whopper lightning bolt.

Mum's food shop has plenty of empty wall space – see where I'm going with this? But there is one snag – the greatest living missing New York abstract expressionist CANNOT have his paintings exhibited in something called a Farm Emporium,

THANK YOU

VERY MUCH!

Z
Z
z

— **PAST MY FLIPPING BEDTIME NEWS** —

I may have just solved all of the Hopkinson family's financial problems. These pictures are going to be a game clanger*.

* GAME CLANGER – mistake in a game which makes a big difference.

CHAPTER 27

ANOTHER LITTLE CHAT WITH GRANDPA

I HAVE BEEN **AGONISING** OVER WHAT TO CALL MY NEW ART GALLERY, BUT IT'S GOING TO BE SOMETHING DEADLY LIKE SPOON - OR CHICKEN - OR SPACE - OR HEAVEN - OR DART (THAT'S A GOOD ONE) - OR CONSCIENCE. YOU SEE WHERE I'M GOING WITH THIS THEME - **REALLY COOL** AND **MOODY** AND **MYSTERIOUS** AND MAKING NO SENSE WHATSOEVER. I THINK IT COULD WORK ON THE ADULTS WHO THINK THEY KNOW STUFF.

But I need to get my cart hitched up to my horse or I will be all hat and no cattle, as they say in North Korea, because I need to get Grandpa to let me be 'his gallery'. (That's how they say it in the business.) After all, they are his pictures.

186

So, while Grandpa and I were going over our selections for that afternoon's racing (don't forget I get a cut of any of the WINNINGS so this is an important part of my day), I slipped my **MAGIC POCKET WATCH** out of my belt and innocently started swinging it in front of his nose – without him really knowing that I was doing it.

'Grandpa...look at my lovely **MAGIC POCKET WATCH** . . . which you will forget you've ever seen . . . backwards and forwards, forwards and backwards.'

'Very nice, Holly . . . where did you get that from? I'm sure I've seen it before . . .'

'No you have NOT, Grandpa,' I said quickly in my 'Spiro, Spero' voice and gave him two verses, which I think will be enough.

'Grandpa . . . by the way, you've never seen this watch before . . . not even in New York . . . but tell me this . . . when you WERE in New York, did you sign your pictures with a funny SQUIGGLE in the bottom left-hand corner?'

'Oh yes . . . always . . . it was your Grandma Esme's idea . . . She didn't think it was a good idea to put my real name on anything . . . in case I wanted to pass it off as someone else's work . . . She was a **CUNNING** one, your grandma.'

'So did you bring all your pictures back from New York?'

'Oh no . . . some dreamer used to take the odd one off me in exchange for eating in their restaurant . . . but that didn't last for long . . .'

So I got my smart mobile phone out and showed Grandpa the picture hanging in Aleeshaa's dad's gallery.

'OH YES,'

he replied, glancing up from the phone. 'Not very good, is it? Your grandmother gave it to someone in exchange for a new kitchen.'

'Well, check this out, Grandpa . . . your pictures are worth a lot more than a kitchen . . . and we're going to display them in my new art gallery.'

'GOOD LORD . . . THAT DOESN'T SOUND LIKE A VERY GOOD IDEA . . . WHERE ON EARTH IS THAT GOING TO BE?'

'Well, this is top secret . . . and I haven't totally sorted it out with Mum yet, but I'm going to display works of art in everyday food-shopping situations . . . so, when you're buying your Brussels sprouts or chicken livers, you can pop a work of art into your shopping basket while you're at it. It's going to be a new movement, Grandpa.'

'Oh dear . . . I'm not sure your mother will be too keen on this idea. She'll think my paintings are rubbish.'

'Excuse you, Grandpa, they are not . . . and Holly Hopkinson (Art Gallery Impresso Inc.) is going to showboat you. Your treasures are safe in my hands.'

'Oh dear . . .' said Grandpa in his 'abstract expressionist' voice.

ALL HOLLY HOPKINSON (ART GALLERY

IMPRESSO INC. IN ASSOCIATION WITH

FILM AND LOCATION PLACES INC.) NEEDS

NOW IS A MAGIC POCKET WATCH

SESSION WITH MY MUM.

CHAPTER 28

CONFRONTING MISS BOSSOM

NOTHING HAS IMPROVED THIS MORNING ON THE SCHOOL BUS À LA SLINKY DAVE. HE IS DRIVING LIKE THE HUNCHBACK OF NOTRA-DAME, AND THE **DARK CLOUD** HANGING OVER HIM LOOKS LIKE TURNING INTO RAIN ANY MINUTE NOW.

So I did not engage him in light conversation of any kind –

not even about the weather.

Vinnie got on the bus at the top of the lane so I dragged him on to the back seats spit-spot and gave him three verses of SPIRO, SPERO.

I was beginning to think I might be too late. So I had to double-whopper pull something out of the bag spit-spot.

'Vinnie . . . you will cause a distraction in the playground outside our classroom when we get to school. Nothing over the top, Vinnie . . . do not take your clothes off or anything like that . . . just enough to get the attention of all the kids, and Felicity Snoop in particular.

Vinnie said, 'All riight,' in his 'slightly confused' voice. But I couldn't spell it out any clearer because we were already at Daffodil's stop.

┌─────────── *UNDERWEAR NEWS* ───────────┐
for the literary record, I DEFO-NIGHTLY said,
'DO NOT take your pants off.'
└──┘

So I crept into our classroom SOTTO VOCE, as they say in Scotland. Miss Bossom was frantically turning the pages of a picture book so, as soon as I heard Vinnie kicking off in the playground, and a few stragglers rushed out to see what was going on, I sneaked up behind her.

She was looking at a catalogue of paintings called *Zombie Formalism*. They looked like someone had made a **TERRIBLE** mess

spilling things

on the floor.

Miss Bossom was sighing and making excited noises just like Barkley does when Mum's about to feed him. So I had to clear my throat and make some pretty odd noises myself (think Aunt Electra swallowing her RAW EGGS) just to get her attention.

'Miss Bossom . . . please look very carefully at my **MAGIC POCKET WATCH**,' I commanded in my 'no-nonsense' voice.

'Not now, Holly . . . I'm very busy scanning the auction-house catalogues,' she replied dismissively in her 'modern-art collector' voice. 'This **ZOMBIE** formalism is just exquisite.'

193

'BUT IT'S A MODERN-ART POCKET WATCH.'

'Oh . . . what period?'

I cut the small talk and waved it furiously forwards and backwards, backwards and forwards, giving her an extra verse because she had sunglasses on!

'Miss Bossom . . . can you hear me?' I enquired, trying to work out whether I had successfully goggle-eyed her.

'Of course I can, you absurd child,' she replied.

'Miss Bossom . . . you are not a modern-art collector . . . you are a slightly weird teacher in Lower Goring . . . do you understand?'

'YES, HOLLY.'

'Good . . .' That was a flipping relief.

'And you are going to marry Slinky Dave in a normal wedding . . . no glass pyramids or rotting turnips on people's heads . . . or any installations or inner sanctums . . .'

'YES, HOLLY.'

'But you're not going back to Mrs Chichester's plans either . . . no pink doves or gold thrones . . . you shall just marry in Lower Goring church with the vicar, if he promises not to wear his firefighter's helmet . . . just a nice RURAL-style wedding.'

'YES, HOLLY.'

'And you will let Slinky Dave put the TV back in the front room . . . and no more modern-art nonsense at home.'

'OK, HOLLY.'

Then I glanced out of the window – to see Vinnie doing the FUNKY CHICKEN walk with his pants on his head followed by the rest of my class in a conga line.

As Miss Bossom was being so obedient, I thought I might as well keep going.

'For your RURAL wedding, Miss Bossom . . . you will invite Felicity Snoop and Daffodil to be flower ducks . . . and you will find a nice roll of honour for me . . .'

I was about to finesse* my official position when the **LUNATIC** Vinnie came crashing into the classroom, trying to escape the conga line who were after his pants.

But I think we can assume JOB DONE by my MAGIC POCKET WATCH.

Normal service is RESUMEO.

CHAPTER 29

MUM AND ELECTRA GO HEAD TO HEAD

SO I WAS **HANGING OUT** IN THE FARMYARD THIS AFTERNOON, MINDING MY OWN BUSINESS WITH MUM AND CHEWING THE CUD, WHEN GUESS WHO CAME BELTING DOWN THE LANE?

YES.

Aunt Electra.

She was hopping **MAD** when she jumped out of her car. Jerking around like a kangaroo with ants in its pants.

'Sally . . . we need to have a word . . . inside . . . now . . . away from young ears,' all the while looking at me and doing **CRAZY** spinning stuff with her ears as if anything's my fault.

So this is the problemo – it turns out that Mum is going to go head to head with Aunt Electra and the Chequers for the coffee-drinking market. And Aunt Electra is NOT happy about it.

'You are meant to be running a farm shop that sells food, not a café that sells cappuccinos,' Aunt Electra said to Mum in the kitchen in her 'outdoor-pub' voice.

'It's an EMPORIUM, if you don't mind . . . and you are supposed to be selling beer and bar food . . . not cappuccinos,' Mum barked in her 'very loud voice which she uses for people from other countries', even though they understand her perfectly well. Grandpa looked up from the *Racing Post*.

'Why aren't either of you selling the *Racing Post*?' he demanded.

'Because you can't eat it,' Mum said in a voice she should not use to Grandpa.

'And another thing . . . I've seen a poster saying you're going to be serving sandwiches made from local produce,' Aunt Electra said, wagging her finger at Mum.

'And what is WRONG with that?' Mum asked.

'That is OUR speciality . . . so WHO is going to supply you?'

'That's a commercial secret,' Mum replied in her 'Mrs Chichester' voice.

'And another thing,' Aunt Electra said, 'why has Vinnie asked for a pay rise . . . because he's "had other offers"?'

'Well, I'm looking for a washer-upper . . . and Vinnie is as entitled to the job as anyone else.'

'Is he, indeed? Well, we'll see about that.'

Then Aunt Electra flounced out of the kitchen like the Charge of the Light Brigade. And Mum's head looked like a turnip that was about to explode into a million pieces all over the place.

Which gave me an 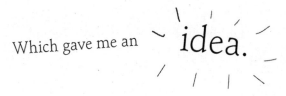 idea.

'Mum,' I said in my 'business' voice, 'you might like to know that I've started up a new agency.'

'Oh really, Holly. What sort of agency?'

'A fixing agency – I fix things – so if you want Vinnie to work for you, I'll fix him, and if you want Vince to sell you local produce I can fix that too. All you have to do is get on to the people in the Amazon and order me an Apple Mac, and I will work exclusively for you in the food and employment area of your business.'

'But I thought you were Grandpa's racing manager?' Mum said.

'Excuse you . . . that is a separate business from Holly Hopkinson (Fixing Agent Inc.).'

'Is it just?' Mum said. 'And which company supplies live farm-emporium-style music?'

'That's Holly Hopkinson (Band Manager Inc.), Mum . . . but you're making this very complicated. If you just deal with me direct, I can sort it all out for you. So would you like to book The Cool?'

'No, I would not. But perhaps one of you could sort Vince out for me because I know what that sneaky aunt of yours is going to do. She's going to try and get him to stop supplying me with local produce.'

'Ah well, as you know, Holly Hopkinson (Film Location and Places Inc.) has a very good relationship with Vince when I have that hat on.'

'Well, I suggest you choose whichever hat you like and get over to Vince's farm lickety-split, young lady.'

Mum can be **very cheeky** when she feels like it – and that may just affect how she comes out in these memoirs if she doesn't wind her neck in, as they say on fishing boats.

— BAD TIMING NEWS —

this was OBVIOUSLY NOT the right moment to offer Mum the great opportunity to host the Gâllèrie de Muséé du Crêdules in her emporium, as she insists on calling it.

Timing is everything in life when you're dealing with twitchy adults, even if you do have a **MAGIC POCKET WATCH** in your belt.

So I went up to see Vince, on official business. He was leaning against his gate, chewing grass and watching Vinnie riding Le Prince round the field.

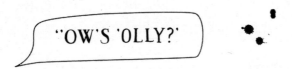

"OW'S 'OLLY?"

Vince asked in his 'hungry farmer' voice.

'Well, running to stand still,' I replied in my 'busy' voice. But Vince looked a bit PUZZLED by that and scratched his head as he thought about it. So I got straight down to work.

Holly Hopkinson (Corporation Head Office) was NOT in the mood to chew grass all day, leaning against a gate.

'Look at my **MAGIC POCKET WATCH**,' I commanded Vince. 'Going backwards and forwards, forwards and backwards.'

'AYE.'

'SPIRO, SPERO, SQUIGGLEOUS SCOTCH, CAST YOUR EYES WHITHER MY WATCH!'

I repeated my mantra three times. Vince is a very good subject as he concentrates like a lizard watching a big fat fly – although Vince's tongue is a bit shorter.

'Vince . . . you are going to supply Mum and the Hopkinson farm shop with all of your fresh produce.'

'Aye . . . all of it? What about the Chequers?'

'Aunt Electra will have to get her stuff from Bohemia . . . and anyway they won't need your stuff. Dad's new menu is going to "fascinate the plates of our gor mays with TEMPTATIONS from around the globe". . . so I don't think that includes your spuds and other stuff.'

'Aye . . . whatever you say, 'Olly . . . fine by me . . . as long as it all goes when I 'ave it, I don't mind.'

'Excellent, Vince . . . I knew you'd see sense . . . and Vince . . . Mum and the farm shop are going to be your exclusive providers of CAPPA-CHINOS at Beastival.'

'Really? I was thinking of getting some straight from Brazil . . . They can stick it on the van from the Amazon.'

'That's out of the question, Vince. You have to go local otherwise Harmony will start protesting about your food miles . . . and **NO PLASTIC CUPS**. Mum will supply you with bio cups that rot while you're drinking your coffee.'

'AYE . . . ALL RIIGHT, 'OLLY . . . **WHATEVER YOU SAY.'**

So I think Mum will be very pleased with my fixing services – and the timing is finally right to have 'the gallery chat' with her.

CHAPTER 30

PREPOSITIONING* MUM

SO WHEN MUM'S ELASTIC-POLYURETHANE-FIBRE-CLAD BOTTOM PUT IN AN APPEARANCE THE NEXT MORNING, LOOKING TO BULK UP WITH AVOCADO MUSH, I POUNCED LIKE A COILED TRAFFIC WARDEN.

'Good morning, Mum,' I said in my 'bright as a button' voice. But I knew she wasn't listening to me cos I'm the least important member of the Hopkinson family, so SHE thinks. But before she knows it I'm going to be like Lycra – all over her.

'How is your architect's therapy going?' I asked.

'Good, thank you, but I'm in a **TERRIBLE** rush,' she replied in her 'not listening' voice.

* PREPOSITIONING – preparing Mum to do as she's told, thank you very much.

So I accidentally dropped the milk jug on the floor to get her attention.

'Whoops.'

'Oh, Holly . . . you clumsy girl,' she said as she bent over to mop up the milk. As I predicted, her Oh Cee Dee is NOT capable of flitting out of the door to Pilates with spilled milk on the floor.

'Look at my **MAGIC POCKET WATCH**, Mum,' I instructed as she dabbed the tiles. And I gave her three verses:

'SPIRO, SPERO, SQUIGGLEOUS SCOTCH, CAST YOUR EYES WHITHER MY WATCH.'

'Mum . . . you are going to say yes to the very generous offer of me hanging the Gâllèrie de Muséé du Crêdules' pictures on your walls.'

'What are you talking about, Holly?'

'My new art gallery, excuse you . . . and it's going to be in your food emporium.'

'Oh . . . well, that's exciting . . . yes . . . of course, Holly.'

Now I was VERY worried about the next bit – so I swung my **MAGIC POCKET WATCH** very slowly and goggled Mum in the eyes with menace.

'And you ARE going to change its name from the Farm Emporium to the Farm Arcade now that you have a gallery in it . . . and this is non-conditioner.'

'Oh . . . I quite like that actually,' Mum said in her 'surprised' voice. 'Yes . . . the Farm Arcade . . . it has a bit of a multi-use air to it.'

'Not too multi, Mum,' I said. 'Don't be getting ideas of letting Mrs Chichester have any acreage in this arcade.'

'OH . . . RIGHTY-HO . . . IT WAS JUST A THOUGHT.'

'Zip it, Mum,' I advised,

BUT THIS DEAL IS A BIG RELIEF. BECAUSE

I WAS LOOKING LIKE BEING ALL PICTURES

AND NO GALLERY WHEN

THE TIDE WENT OUT.

Holly Hopkinson (Art Gallery Impresso Inc.) is
up and running in the art world – and that is

OFFICIAL.

CHAPTER 31

HARMONY BACK ON THE MARCH

JUST WHEN I DIDN'T NEED ANY NONSENSE FROM THE COOL – IT ALL KICKED OFF IN THE RECORDING-STUDIO SHED.

Harmony has been focusing on writing love ballads for them to perform – which I think may be because she's still BOGGLE-EYED with Stickly – but Shovel is NOT HAPPY with such soppy rubbish, and he says he might quit the band.

So Harmony has walked off the job – which is DOUBLE-WHOPPER *BAD NEWS* for me on two of my business fronts.

1. On the Holly Hopkinson (Band Manager Inc.) front – I just don't need this.

2. Harmony is planning on setting up a demonstration outside the Farm Arcade so that is not good news for Holly Hopkinson (Art Gallery Impresso Inc.). It will play havoc with my footfall, and I've got two old tractor engines ready to palm off on some

   DOOFUSES.

'Excuse you,' I said to Harmony, 'but WHY are you planning to demonstrate? There aren't any new houses being built near the flipping Farm Arcade.'

'Remember . . . I'm, like, sooo vegan?' Harmony replied in her 'teenager' voice.

'So you keep saying, but you and Stickly were drinking CAPPA-CHINOS in Chipping Topley yesterday,' I pointed out.

'Well . . . they, like, sooo had soya milk in them.'

'Look, Harmony, I am a modern band manager and art gallery impresso, and I agree that we shouldn't eat animals. So why not do a massive vegan demonstration at Beastival? Not here – Mum's biggest-selling items are vegetables, you double-whopper doofus.'

Harmony looked totally foxed.

'Yeah . . . but, like . . . Mum's vegetables are sooo, like, unsustainable.'

'And how do you figure that out?'

'Because Vince, like, uses CARBON FUEL in his tractor . . . and he supplies Mum.'

'EXCELLENTO,' I said in my 'Italian' voice. 'In that case you can flipping well give Vince double rations of protesting then. Mum's hardly flying roses in from Kenya, is she?'

'YOU'RE BEING, LIKE, **SOOO UNCOOL** NOW, HOLLY.'

'Excuse you, where do you think that rose that Stickly gave you came from last week – Kent? In the winter? I don't think so!'

Anyway, I could see that I was getting nowhere, so it was time to give her a dose of my **MAGIC POCKET WATCH.**

'Look at my lovely **MAGIC POCKET WATCH,** Harmony.'

'Basic . . . like . . . where did you get that from? It's sooo cool.'

'That . . . MON VICTOR BRAVO* . . . is for me to know and you to wonder,' as they say in Greece.

'Just look at it going backwards and forwards, forwards and backwards,' and then I recited just two verses.

* **MON VICTOR BRAVO** – what the French say when they're even more terrified.

'SPIRO, SPERO, SQUIGGLEOUS SCOTCH,
CAST YOUR EYES WHITHER MY WATCH.'

'Harmony ... you will not protest outside Mum's Farm Arcade while Holly Hopkinson (Art Gallery Impresso Inc.) has a gallery in there ...

OK? IT'S **VERY BAD** FOR MY BUSINESS.'

'Like ... OK, Holly,' Harmony said in her 'sooo unfair' voice.

I cannot have my goofy older sister re-railing my financial survivalist plan. Which involves selling pictures for a lot more than turnips or out-of-date yoghurt.

CHAPTER 32

THE GRAND OPENING

MUM HAS LOST THE PLOT! I MEAN, I KNOW MY MAGIC POCKET WATCH AND I TOLD HER TO MAKE SURE HER SHOP WAS NOTHING LIKE MRS CHICHESTER'S 'EMPORIUM OF BAD TASTE', AS DAD CALLS IT, BUT I DID NOT INTEND HER TO GO BONKERS.

Who has ever double-whopper heard of a Farm Arcade that has:

- a helicopter landing pad 

- people running around in black shirts and trousers, speaking into microphones
- a special car-wash area for black Range Rovers only
- personal shoppers to choose your turnips for you
- valet parking?

I have to agree that my mother knows a bit about PR stuff, but I think she's lost it — and imagine having an EDGY art gallery with that sort of carry-on going on all around you?

If I don't watch her onions, my Gâllèrie de Muséé du Crêdules will be the laughing stock of the art-gallery world.

Anyway the **NEW PRESS NEWS** is that Mum is having a press-preview evening — and I think it's fair to say that, because Mum used to be such a SUPREMO in the PR world, both my new friend from the *Daily Chipping Topley Mail* and the woman from RoundaboutChippingTopley.com are coming.

The Gâllèrie de Muséé du Crêdules is obviously very much part of the press evening, and Grandpa's pictures are hanging in the following areas of the food sheds: vegetables, meat counter, cheese cupboard, dairy (refrigerated) and bread.

But, after a chance visit to Dad's cricketing butcher friend Sir Garfield's backyard, I was able to source all sorts of other stuff that sells for a fortune in Notting Hill galleries: half an old plough, a milking machine (retired), a broken **CHAINSAW**, a post-basher, a broken fork and an old tractor engine that looks much better than the car engine in Aleeshaa's dad's gallery – and Sir Garfield has lots more of these works of art that I can sell in the future, so I have no shortage of stock.

I've spread them all round the food sheds in what Aleeshaa would call 'random' places. When Harmony arrived, I think she was most impressed. She just said, 'That's, like, sooo basic . . .' I don't think praise comes any higher than that.

So Mum gave my new friend from the *Daily Chipping Topley Mail* and the woman from the RoundaboutChippingTopley.com website loads of grub to eat – in fact, I've never seen two people scoff so much food in all my life – and they took samples home of **DAMAGED** stock in party bags. If you like free food, it seems journalism is a good job to get into.

My new friend from the *Daily Chipping Topley Mail* asked me QUITE a lot of questions. I would say he's more like their art correspondent than their Farm Arcade food writer.

So this is going to be good for the Gâllèrie de Muséé du Crêdules. I did think about taking him behind the free-standing turnip display while I was explaining all about Grandpa and how he's one of the lost wonders of the world, but the guy was smiling and nodding and letting me talk so much I didn't think it was necessary to complicate matters by bringing out my

MAGIC POCKET WATCH.

Like Mum, he was a bit slow on the **COMPRENDO** appreciating the 'broken mechanical theme' from Sir Garfield's backyard so I had to spell out the clever arty bit to him.

'You see, the exhibits between the food displays on the floor of the shop – I mean the gallery's horizontal-display areas – represent the contrast between the mechanisation synonymous with farm machinery and the rural landscape that the food is produced in,' I told him in my 'bigged-up' voice.

You wait and see – there will be Range Rovers from Notting Hill backed up along the hard shoulder of the M40 looking to buy up the contents of Sir Garfield's backyard. Dick Whittington's cat will want to watch itself, the way they drive.

Not that I shall EVER reveal the source of my art – after all, you don't hear Tracey Ermine telling everyone where she gets her fur and cutlery from when she's doing her creations.

'Really? Well, that's all very interesting,' my friend and confidant from the *Mail* kept saying in his 'interested' voice.

'Is there anything else you'd like to know about Grandpa in New York? Of course, if he hadn't had to come home to see Dad, he'd have been world-famous now,' I said in my 'media-friendly' voice.

'Yes . . . of course . . . what a pity. So no trouble in New York then?'

It was nice of him to ask, but no one had mentioned any trouble to me so I used one of Mum's PR tricks and just denied it, even though I had no idea whether there had been or not.

'No trouble at all . . . just a bit homesick. So, when might I expect to read your review?' I asked.

'Oh, in a couple of days. I just need to do some digging around,' he replied.

'Well, I wouldn't bother to focus too much on the root-vegetable side of things,' I advised. He could be days unearthing swedes – I needed this piece on the newspaper stands.

'Oh, just one other thing,' he said in his 'sneaky' voice. 'Why Gâllèrie de Muséé du Crêdules?'

'EXCUSE YOU?'

'Why is your, er . . . display . . . you know . . . I mean gallery, called Gâllèrie de Muséé du Crêdules?'

Typical **PESKY** journalist – just when you think you've fed them all the doings they need to hear, they then produce a tripwire. I couldn't exactly admit the name was to suck in all my fellow avant-gardeys from Notting Hill, could I? In case he blows the lid right off its flipping hinges in his pesky paper.

'Ah yes . . . Gâllèrie de Muséé du Crêdules. Well, you see, it represents the relationship between . . .' I looked across the room, searching for perspiration – and saw a big pile of onions. 'Yes, it represents the connection between the soil of England and France, which has been at the heart of so much **ARTISTIC TENSION** over the years.'

He smiled and swallowed it into his notebook like a baby starling GOBBLING down worms from its mother's beak.

CHAPTER 33

MRS SMARTSIDE HITS THE DECK

THINGS ARE GETTING PRETTY BUSY
IN THE FARM ARCADE – BUT IT IS NOT
ALL ROSY IN THE VEGETABLE PATCH,
I CAN TELL YOU.

So Mrs Smartside and her friend the Hon. Eleanor Higginbottom-Smythe were in the Farm Arcade just having a snoop around, if you ask me, because they hadn't requested the assistance of a personal shopper or one of the bristling black shirts – and Mrs Smartside had her yappy dogs with her, which shouldn't be allowed because I know what they do over the sprouts that are at dog-leg level.

Anyway, Moggy very much feels that the Farm Arcade is her 'manor' as she IS still the farm cat, even if she's having to up her game a bit.

Well, Mrs Smartside's yappy dogs got a sniff of Moggy somewhere near the tinned tomatoes, and they took off after her.

Mrs Smartside ended up doing an impression of a champagne cork coming out of a bottle as she was dragged after them (probably a Nebuchadnezzar* cork rather than a regular one).

The Hon. Eleanor Higginbottom-Smythe was squeezing an avocado to see if it was ripe, and she was not prepared for the shove that she got from Mrs Smartside as she rocketed past.

So it wasn't my fault that the Hon. Eleanor Higginbottom-Smythe fell backwards, flinging the avocado like a flipping hand **GRENADE** in the process, and got wedged on top of Sir Garfield's tractor engine, which was minding its own business. She should count herself lucky it wasn't the broken fork.

* NEBUCHADNEZZAR – a large bottle that holds twenty normal bottles of champagne, named after a king of Babylon who was a bit on the thirsty side due to the hot weather in the desert.

The people in the black shirts with their microphones could not shift her, so the fire brigade had to be called. I've never seen such a fuss in all my life.

The Hon. Eleanor Higginbottom-Smythe was hollering her head off and threatening immediate additional noise from her lawyers. So, while everyone was trying to untangle Mrs Smartside and her yapping dogs from the cabbage display, I took the opportunity to get my **MAGIC POCKET WATCH** out and 'cook' the Hon. Eleanor Higginbottom-Smythe.

'The Hon. Eleanor Higginbottom-Smythe, will you look at my **MAGIC POCKET WATCH,** please?'

'GO AWAY, YOU WRETCHED CHILD!'

she shouted in her 'not very child-friendly' voice.

'Backwards and forwards, forwards and backwards,' I chanted.

And then I gave her five verses of **SPIRO, SPERO.**

223

'The Hon. Eleanor Higginbottom-Smythe, you are going to insist that it was all your fault getting wedged on top of one of the tractor engine sculptures,' I commanded. 'And, what is more, you now like it so much you are going to buy it . . . SOTTO PROMPTO . . . as soon as the firefighters have winched you off it.'

'I will, young lady.'

'And you will forget you have ever met me or my **MAGIC POCKET WATCH.**'

'WELL, WHO EXACTLY ARE YOU?'

'EXCELLENT,'

I replied, comforted by such a prompt lack of memory.

So Holly Hopkinson (Art Gallery Impresso Inc.) has made her first sale – this is a very good sign that there's a thriving art market in the Chipping Topley and Lower Goring area.

CHAPTER 34

THE REVIEW

SO GRANDPA IS STILL NOT TOO HAPPY ABOUT ME PUTTING ALL OF HIS PICTURES UP IN THE FOOD SHEDS.

'I don't know why you want to go dragging all of this back up . . . No one's interested in this sort of painting these days,' Grandpa moaned.

'Grandpa, that is where you're wrong, I can assure you. You are going to get quite a shock when everyone gets an even bigger shock that you are the most FAMOUS lost-artist link in the world.'

'What are you talking about, Holly? You sound like your Aunt Electra when she's had too much coffee.'

225

So I decided it was time to spill the beans that I had up my sleeve and let them hatch.

'Grandpa, there's a major gallery in London that has one of your paintings, and they have identified your squiggle as the mark of one of the lost wonders of the New York art scene. So, when Mr de Medici-Smith comes down here and sees this lot, it's going to be double-whopper bingo lift-off time.'

'OH DEAR ...'

'What do you mean "oh dear"?'

'WELL, I DON'T WANT ANY TROUBLE.'

'What makes you think there'll be any trouble, pray INFORMO?'

'Well, the thing is ... I did leave New York under a bit of a cloud.'

His words dropped on to the kitchen floor like one of Vera's Christmas puddings.

'Excuse you ... you left New York under a bit of a cloud? Can you explain, *SIEVE YOU PRAY*, Grandpa?'

'Well, you see, New York was full of mobsters . . . and I started hanging out with the Gambino family at the racetrack. But their horses were slower than their food trucks, and one thing led to another . . . They didn't like my paintings much and therefore wouldn't take them as payment. So your grandma said we should leave and cut our losses . . . on the next boat!'

I WAS NOT expecting that, *mee* thank you VERY much.

But luckily the Hopkinson family have a wealth of PR experience, and we know how to brush stuff under the carpet – even if it is fish and it starts to **PONG** a bit after a few days.

'Well, luckily that DOOFUS from the *Daily Chipping Topley Mail* won't know about any of that jiggery-pokery,' I assured him in my 'PR' voice. 'And he owes me a favour on the back of a biscuit-fight story that Holly Hopkinson (PR Inc.) may have alerted him to so it's not going to be a **PROBLEMO,** as they say in Italy.'

227

I keep meaning to ask Grandpa about Grandma Esme, but I get the feeling that he doesn't want to talk about her.

— PRESS NEWS —

guess who came through the door like the pony expresso waving the *Racing Post* and the *Daily Chipping Topley Mail* around like a lunatic with an outbreak of turtles in his pants?

- YES. -

'I'll take the *Daily Chipping Topley Mail,* thank you very much, Vinnie,' I said in my 'polite but firm' voice and spit-spot skedaddled up to my bedroom.

Thank flipping heck I was sitting down when I read the FRONT PAGE headlines.

NEW YORK ARTIST WITH
MOBSTER
CONNECTIONS UNMASKED IN
LOWER GORING

Scandal rocked the sleepy village of Lower Goring, just a mile from Chipping Topley, this week when it was revealed that an associate of the infamous Gambino mafia family has been living there as a humble farmer.

'He just seems like an ordinary bloke,' one shocked local who wished to remain anonymous said yesterday.

Horatio Hopkinson, 87, had his identity revealed when his very average paintings were strangely used to decorate the new farm shop in Lower Goring . . .

Well, I just couldn't read on – until my eye caught another headline on the next page.

GÂLLÈRIE DE MUSÉÉ DU
CRÊDULES BEYOND A JOKE

The concept of combining a ridiculously pretentious art gallery with a food shop is something that the unsuspecting grocery shoppers of Lower Goring will find not only a physical health-and-safety hazard, but also an insult to their intelligence . . .

And to think that I thought he was a trusted NEW friend who I have helped with biscuit-fight stories – let alone all the food he ate – I even slipped him some extra tempura prawns that everyone was after. I SHALL NOT be making that mistake again,

thank YOU

very much.

This is, without doubt, the **WORST** review that anything put on by Holly Hopkinson (Art Gallery Impresso Inc.) has EVER received. It could bring the whole show down if Grandpa sees it – he'll have those pictures off the wall and on the bonfire before you can say 'Guy Fawkes'.

It was a **DARK HOUR**, but I needed to hold my nerve and cause a distraction. I was going to have to 'throw Dad under a bus', as they say in Oxford, where cars are banned from the city centre.

So I rang the *Daily Chipping Topley Mail* and asked to speak to the news desk.

'Hello,' I said in my 'disguised' voice. 'Can I speak to the food correspondent, please? I have some hot food *BREAKING NEWS.'*

'Well, that's probably me,' he said at the other end of the phone – so I knew who he was, but he didn't know who I was. 'Who's speaking, please?'

'Oh . . . well, I can't reveal my sources, but I have it on good authority that the Sannakji tasting went horribly wrong at the Chequers in Lower Goring last night . . .'

'What is Sannakji?'

'It's a Korean dish . . . and Dad – I mean Mr Hopkinson – was feeding some to Vinnie, who apparently is a local urchin who washes the dishes in the pub, and the Sannakji, which is actually live octopus, bolted from Vinnie's plate and escaped into the river . . . Who knows where it's heading now.'

> 'VERY GOOD . . . ER . . . SORRY, BUT WHO ARE YOU?'

'The same person who wanted to remain anonymous in another story you did this week involving custard creams and other flavours,' I replied. 'Good day to you.'

So I think I've successfully knocked Grandpa off the front pages – now I need to get Mr de Medici-Smith down to the Gâllèrie de Muséé du Crêdules SPIT-DOUBLE-WHOPPER-SPOT sharpish to make me some offers I won't refuse.

I texted Aleeshaa.

HIYA, I HAVE SOME RANDOM MASSIVE NEWS FOR YOUR DAD. PLS TELL HIM I HAVE CLIENT WITH PAINTINGS BY THE NEW YORK ARTIST WHO DOES THE SQUIGGLE IN THE LEFT-HAND CORNER BUT HE NEEDS TO BE QUICK
X

NOT COOL 😕 DAD HAS BEEN ARRESTED BY THE ART POLICE FOR HAVING FORGERIES IN HIS GALLERY – SOME MIX-UP – THEY TOOK EVERYTHING FROM THE GALLERY ...

It took a while for this bombshell to land on my head and go off – of course it's terrible for Monsieur de Medici-Smith and Aleeshaa that there has been this mix-up – but it isn't great for Holly Hopkinson (Art Gallery Impresso Inc.) either, thank you very much.

Because my plan was that a) Aleeshaa's dad was going to swoop on Lower Goring and discover Grandpa, and b) even though Grandpa says he would never sell any of his pictures, Holly Hopkinson (Art Gallery Impresso Inc.) might release one or two on to the market for collectors to fight over.

But now that plan has gone for a burton, and I am in deep DOODOO up to my boots on both legs and an arm. But I need another plan cos:

1. I have to make sure Grandpa doesn't get to see the *Daily Chipping Topley Mail.*

2. Now I have no way of getting Grandpa discovered – or should I say excavated?

3. There is one more BIG ISSUE burning a hole in my pants – was Aleeshaa's dad just spinning me a double-whopper yarn to big up the value of his picture?!!! Or – even double-whopper worse – his flipping forgery?

I thought being an art gallery impresso was going to be easy compared to being a band manager.

—— **BREAKING MOBSTER NEWS** – ——
the farmhouse telephone line rang today and, as usual, I was the one nearest. So I answered it. I had the fright of my LIFE when an American voice demanded, 'Can I speak to Horatio Hopkinson?'

'Excuse you . . . but to whom am I speaking?' I said in my 'telephone-answering' voice.

'It's Mr Gambino here,' the voice said.

'Oh,' I replied. 'Well, he is indisposed at the moment so you'll need to call back when he isn't in again.'

And then the penny dropped.

'And if I was you, Mr Gambino,' I continued, 'I'd spit-spot to your flipping recording shed and stop annoying me, thank you **very** much.'

My brother thinks he's very funny. One day events and my **MAGIC POCKET WATCH** will catch up with him. And he'll be walking around using a **BOG SEAT** as a permanent hat.

CHAPTER 35

EXCLUSIVE CHAT WITH AUNT ELECTRA

EVEN THOUGH THE PLATES OF HOLLY HOPKINSON (CORPORATION HEAD OFFICE) ARE SPINNING OUT OF FLIPPING CONTROL, SOMETHING TELLS ME I NEED TO GET TO THE BOTTOM OF THE GRANDMA ESME STORY IF I'M EVER GOING TO UNDERSTAND GRANDPA'S LIFE – BUT HE ISN'T GOING TO SPIT-SPOT GALLOP HIS SPILLED BEANS ANYWHERE NEAR MY FLIPPING PLATE. THAT'S DARK HORSES FOR YOU, THANK YOU VERY MUCH.

But I think his daughter, otherwise known as my Aunt Electra, might if I catch her à la carte in the right mood, relaxing in MY Arabian tent with a large pink martini clinking in her hand.

'Have you seen how shiny my **MAGIC POCKET WATCH** is, Aunt Electra?' I asked her in my 'innocent' voice, as I cuddled up to her on a massive BOHEMIAN cushion.

'Nice try, Holly, but don't even think about using that on me . . .'

'Of course not, Aunt Electra. I just wanted you to see how well I'm looking after it for future generations.'

'What do you want? I know Holly Hopkinson doesn't give away free cuddles when she's in her office.'

'EXCUSE YOU, I AM KNOWN FOR MY FREE HUGGING, THANK YOU VERY MUCH . . . IF YOU HUMOUR ME A LITTLE BIT.'

'AND ...?'

'Well, I was wondering . . . you know . . . well, what happened to Grandma Esme. Has she gone to heaven?'

'HEAVEN? WHAT ON EARTH MAKES YOU THINK SHE'S GONE TO HEAVEN?'

'Well, she's not here . . . and Dad, you and Grandpa never really talk about her so, you know . . . ?'

'Darling, your grandmother didn't go to heaven. She went to Vegas with the bandleader from the club we used to hang out in.'

'Whaaat? No one's ever mentioned this before to my ears,' I pointed out in my 'very affronted' voice.

'No, well, it's not exactly fireside-chat-with-the-vicar sort of information, is it?'

'What made her flipping well do that?'

'Oh, I don't really know, but she didn't like your grandpa wandering off round New York – going to the racetrack and hanging out with **GANGSTERS** – so she kept trying to use your **MAGIC POCKET WATCH** to keep him at home, but it didn't work. I guess the watch knew that it might be good for my dad to get inspiration for his painting by going to those places . . . although it didn't seem to work much.'

'But Grandpa said it was Grandma who insisted that he double-whopper brought all his paintings home.'

'His paintings . . . right. Yes, she got us all packed up – crates of the pictures and whatever valuable possessions we had – and settled your grandpa and me into our cabins on the cruise liner.'

'TO LONDON?'

'Er . . . I think it was Liverpool actually, and, as we waved goodbye to the crowd on the quay, there she was, waving goodbye with the rest of them.'

'Maybe she forgot something and went back for it?'

'No, she didn't forget anything, but she went back for the bandleader . . . and on my bunk she'd left a letter saying she'd come and find me soon and explained how the **MAGIC POCKET WATCH** would look after me.'

'BLIMEY, GRANDPA MUST HAVE BEEN FLIPPING LIVID!'

'Um . . . well, he was a bit upset to say goodbye to the bandleader, who was very good, but he was pretty relaxed about Grandma going to Vegas. He said the weather was nice there.'

Well, you could have knocked me over with a garbage truck – as they say in downtown New York – you just don't expect your grandparents to carry on like that, do you? And that is a rheumatoidical* question,

thank you

very much.

I am beginning to wonder if I have been born into a reality-TV-show family.

* RHEUMATOIDICAL – disorderly question that doesn't have an answer.

CHAPTER 36

THE GUY FROM THE COUNCIL

YOU **WILL NOT BELIEVE** WHO CAME INTO THE FARM ARCADE TODAY, OR SHOULD I SAY THE GÂLLÈRIE DE MUSÉÉ DU CRÊDULES? I AM BEGINNING TO THINK THAT MY SCULPTURES ARE PULLING IN **MORE** PEOPLE THAN MUM'S CHEESES, WHICH ARE BEGINNING TO **WHIFF** OF BAD SOCKS LIKE THE CHANGING ROOMS (BOYS) AT MY **LONDON** SCHOOL.

As soon as I saw him, I knew that I knew him from somewhere if you know what I mean – and you can't miss his orange safety glasses.

'Excuse you . . . did you deliver the coal to Vince's farm the other day?' I asked in my 'rather disarming cute girl' voice. 'Aren't you the . . .' But he seemed to be talking about coal, or the environment, or something in a 'far-off' voice. So that pretty well ruled him out as Vince's coal merchant – which is who I thought he was.

Then it occurred to me that some busybody nosy parker like Felicity Snoop might have reported 'the Hon. Eleanor Higginbottom-Smythe incident' to the authorities – so, if I'm not careful, I'll be in trouble with the council for fly-tipping rubbish and scrap metal all over the place.

I needed to get my guard up, tie-quon-doe style, before he could have me locked up.

'You're from the council, aren't you?' I enquired. 'Because my artists don't take kindly to being accused of dumping stuff round the Farm Arcade.'

'YOU KNOW YOU DON'T BECOME AN "ARTIST" UNLESS YOU'VE GOT A SOUL,'

the guy from the council insisted.

'Excuse you,' I replied in my 'very offended' voice. 'We don't do fish in this part of the arcade . . .'

'As it happens, I have quite a large collection of them,' the guy from the council boasted. 'And I see you do too . . .'

Well, I was about to have him escorted off the premises by the black shirts, who were momentarily busy pointing people to the frozen-yoghurt section, when I was flattened by a tuna sandwich* of screaming children, including some of my classmates.

Gaspar, Tiger and Wolfe came careering up as if it was National Idiot Day, with Crocus, Amaryllis and Iris on their tail. Daffodil (the traitor) and Felicity Snoop weren't far behind.

And they were all **desperate** to get a photo with the guy from the council in his orange safety glasses.

They were all shouting at him.

---

* **TUNA SANDWICH** – a huge wave of children eating lunch.

IT'S FLIPPING WELL 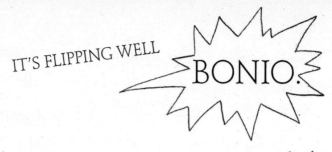 BONIO.

Luckily there was such chaos that nobody – including Bonio – realised that I hadn't known that Bonio was Bonio. And I'm excusing myself for thinking he was from the council.

Put yourself in MY situation. If you're standing next to a pile of whiffing Brussels sprouts at a Farm Arcade, who is more likely to walk past you? A bloke from the council poking his nose into something he doesn't need to smell or Bonio, the most famous band person in the world?

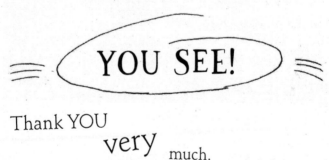 YOU SEE!

Thank YOU very much.

Anyway, he seemed very keen to talk to me IN PRIVATE about Grandpa's pictures, and this REALLY BIGGED me up in front of Daffodil.

So I facilitated her to hang out with me and Bonio, in a minor capacity, of course, but I made it very clear that he didn't want to be crowded by anyone else.

So it wasn't my fault that Felicity Snoop had to sling her hook; mush; spit-spot to somewhere else; vamoose; scarper; ⟶ EXITO EXPRESSO.

'By the way, I knew you were famous all along . . . I was just having you on,' I said to Bonio. 'And, by the way, I know Andrew Lord Webber and Steven Speedberg . . . and the queen . . . so I'm not that impressed, OK? Holly Hopkinson's the name, by the way. Pardon my French.'

'So, Holly, you know when you first become famous you start walking a little differently because people stare at you?' he said in his 'rock star' voice.

'Oh, are you sure it isn't because you're wearing very strange shoes?' I asked in my 'diplomatic' voice. Because Bonio has secret compartments in the bottom of his shoes – probably to keep money in.

245

But I don't think he heard me.

'These paintings are terrific – the real deal – but how did you get them?' Bonio asked, his eyes gleaming behind his safety glasses, as he looked at Grandpa's pictures.

'Well, the Gâllèrie de Muséé du Crêdules has quite a close relationship with the artist. It could be a him or a her, of course. I'm not revealing anything.'

'Oh, it's a him all right. I know his work – I even have one of his pieces. He's one of the lost treasures of the world. Can I meet him?'

Bonio was really animated – he was waving his arms around and jumping up and down a bit on his springy shoes.

THIS NEWS

made me so excited I thought my ears were going to blow off. Double-whopper flipping heck – this was the breakthrough that Holly Hopkinson (Art Gallery Impresso Inc.) has been waiting for ALL MY GALLERY LIFE!

And I was just about to blow Grandpa's cover and take Bonio over to watch the racing with him when Holly Hopkinson (Band Manager Inc.) stepped in.

'Well, that's what everyone says,' she said. I could NOT believe my ears, even though the words were coming out of my mouth. And I knew, if ever there was a moment to fish my **MAGIC POCKET WATCH** out, this was tickety-boo it.

For GOOD and FUN!

'Bonio . . . look at my **MAGIC POCKET WATCH,**' I commanded.

'That's not my name,' he said in his 'grumpy' voice.

'Of course it isn't . . . no one is really called that . . . just keep watching my **MAGIC POCKET WATCH,** backwards and forwards, forwards and backwards.'

And I gave him four verses of **SPIRO, SPERO** – as I had no idea what effect the safety glasses would have on stopping me 'cooking' him.

'Bonio . . . for starters, you will not worry about what I or anyone else call you. We love you anyway.'

'YES, HOLLY.'

'Now, if you want to meet the famous lost New York abstract expressionist, you are going to have to do me a favour.'

'YES, HOLLY . . . ANYTHING YOU SAY . . .'

'OK . . . well, this is the deal. You might like to play with my brother's band THE COOL live at Beastival.'

'You're kidding me . . . when I said ANYTHING, I wasn't going that far . . . no way.'

For a minute, I was worried that my MAGIC POCKET WATCH wasn't working, but then I realised that I had only given him a suggestion – not a COMMAND. So I HAD to be more *direct.*

'Bonio . . . you ARE going to play live with The Cool at Beastival . . . They may not be the greatest, but I'm getting them there,' I said reassuringly in my 'white lie' voice.

'Yeah, Holly,' Bonio said in his **'HORRIFIED'** voice. 'I suppose most people's best work is when they don't know what they're doing.'

"EXCELLENTO . . . you will be in familiar company then,' I said.

A little bird tells me that the ever-twisting fortunes of the Hopkinson family may be back on track – and this is going to put me way above the cappa-chino galleries in Notting Hill.

CHAPTER 37

MISS BOSSOM AND SLINKY DAVE'S 'RURAL' WEDDING

I JUST **DON'T KNOW** WHAT GOT INTO MISS BOSSOM'S HEAD – AND I CAN REPORT THAT MRS CHICHESTER IS LIVID, **SIMPLY LIVID,** ABOUT IT.

No ONE has ever seen anything like it – and I think it may well get into all the wrong magazines. You can forget *Wedding Monthly* and *Bonjour* – they won't be touching the flipping wedding pictures with a bargepole in the middle of a canal! But it might feature in *Plough and Tractor* or *Muck Spreader Monthly*.

'Has this got anything to do with you?' Aunt Electra asked me in her 'accusing' voice when the bride and groom arrived at the church in their pig outfits.

'Excuse YOU,' I replied. 'Do I look like I want to spend the afternoon dressed up as "first turkey"?'

And the vicar didn't seem too happy about having to dress up as a shepherd – so he needs to brush up a bit on his New Testament. WHAT do they teach them at Vicar School these days, I ask you?

'WE decided to have a RURAL-themed wedding,' Bossy Bossom was reported as saying in the *Daily Chipping Topley Mail*. 'We didn't want anything flash . . . like glass pyramids or pink doves.'

But the biggest flipping loser was Holly Hopkinson (Film Location and Places Inc.) because the Chequers and the Farm Arcade both missed out on staging the wedding reception. So also double-whopper bad news for Holly Hopkinson (Band Manager Inc.).

So guess where Bossy and Slinky Dave had their reception?

They only spit-spot double-whopper well had it in the ruins of Lower Goring Hall. I don't suppose health and safety were too **flipping** impressed with that when they both heard about it!

It won't come as any surprise to you that the ruins don't have any electric sockets so that was GOODNIGHT, POMPEII as far as THE COOL being able to play.

And we all got wet feet cos no one has mown the grass for five years – not even Slinky Dave's ex-TV replacement could sort that out.

I mean, how am I meant to work with these

adults?

CHAPTER 38

BONIO RENEGOTIATES

IT TURNS OUT THAT BONIO KNOWS HOW TO NEGOTIATE – AND, IF I'M HONEST, I'M NOT A HUNDRED PER CENT SURE THAT THE 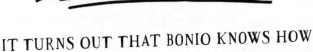 MAGIC POCKET WATCH ACTUALLY GOGGLE-EYED HIM IN THE FIRST PLACE – PERHAPS HE'S PROTECTED BY HIS SAFETY GLASSES? I THINK HE'S JUST PLAYING ALONG WITH ME SO HE CAN MEET THE GREAT LOST ABSTRACT EXPRESSIONIST PAINTER.

So he turns up at the recording shed this morning, not minding his own business, and starts telling the world how it revolves.

'You,' he said, pointing to Shovel. 'I don't want to hear one word coming out of your mouth, OK? I'll do the singing . . . and everything else for that matter.'

Then he turned his attention to Stickly. 'And who are you?'

'STICKLY.'

'Well, cut out all that stretching nonsense. Who do you think you are . . . a Pilates teacher?'

'And you?' he asked, looking at Harold.

'I'm Harold,' squeaked my brother in his **'TERRIFIED'** voice.

'Well, keep the noise down with those drums, OK?'

Harold nodded quietly.

'SO WHERE'S THAT HOLLY?'

Because I'm small and stealthy, as well as being a TERRIFIC band manager, I can keep myself well hidden until I decide to break cover. So I was right behind Bonio and I gave him a right jump when I crept up on him.

'At your service,' I announced.

Bonio and I went for a walk round the farmyard, and he put it to me straight.

'I want to meet him . . . and I want to meet him now,' he declared.

'Well, I hope you like racing then cos you're going to spend the next two hours watching it before he'll even talk to you. And, by the way, he won't have a clue who you are so get over yourself spit-spot now.'

'Good by me,' Bonio said without a care in the world.

CHAPTER 39

RUN-UP TO BEASTIVAL

IT LOOKS LIKE BEASTIVAL IS GOING TO BE BIG – VINCE HAS GOT A POSTER UP BY THE RAILWAY STATION SO EVERYONE KNOWS ABOUT IT. AND VINNIE SAYS THAT BARKLEY WANTS TO GO WITH HIM AS THERE'S GOING TO BE A LOT OF FAST FOOD FLYING AROUND AT SPIT-SPOT TOP SPEED.

PROTEST NEWS –

there are going to be two double-whopper major protests outside the gates of Beastival, according to my sources.

1. The new people from Chipping Topley who are Stickly's neighbours in the new Olde Worlde houses are going to protest against the noise and disturbance caused by Beastival.

2. Harmony and her friends on social media (who she's never met) are going to protest about the exploitation of animals being brought to Beastival. But what about the animals who WANT to go, like Barkley?

Do they get a <u>flipping</u> say?

One of the new Olde Worlde housing urban lot came into the Chequers, looking for support.

'We moved out of Chipping Topley to get some peace and quiet,' he moaned to Dad.

'Would you like to try today's special?' Dad asked him in his 'celebrity chef' voice, taking not a jot of notice of what the noisy customer was whingeing about.

'What is it?'

'Khash . . . very popular in South Asia. Electra and I think it will be a big hit here too.'

'Yes, I'm sure it will be . . . but what is it?'

'Um, good question. It's basically the head, feet and stomach of a cow or sheep . . . cooked nice and slowly overnight.'

'Have you got a licence for that?' the urban whinger bleated.

But Dad isn't as laid-back as he used to be so he spit-spot booted the **MENACE** out of the pub double-whopper foot-up-backside style, as they say in the chef business.

I didn't think Grandpa was going to be too happy about meeting Bonio – cos he doesn't seem to like talking about his pictures, and he isn't interested in bands. But the chat with Bonio has really perked Grandpa up. He's even started wearing a handkerchief round his neck the whole time, and he's walking a bit differently.

And this is Bonio's plan. He is going to pool the picture that he has and the pictures that Gâllèrie de Muséé du Crêdules have, and we're going to have a double-whopper exhibition at Beastival.

I was sure Grandpa wouldn't be up for it, but Bonio has really fired him up.

IN OTHER NEWS -

things are not going well for Harmony on the protesting front.

1. Her friends on social media that she's never even met have turned up, and they are a very unsavoury bunch. Even Dad wouldn't put that lot on his gourmet global food festival menu.

2. Because Harmony's protest camp is next door to the new Olde Worlde Housing urban whingers' protest camp, it looks like she's joining in with their protest – and thus protesting against her boggle-eyed Stickly playing with THE COOL.

So Harmony has had to abandon her protesting career with immediate effect – and, with the help of Moggy, she has gone to Beastival. But, if she thought that was an end to her troubles, she is much mistaken.

Dad has got a stall selling 'Swedish pancakes'*. And he's managed to recruit Harmony to hand out samples. But Mum and the Farm Arcade have the next-door stall, and she wants Harmony to hand out samples of kale-and-Brussels-sprout shots.

--- **HISTORY LESSON NEWS** ---
DURING THE GOLD RUSH IN AMERICA, THE PEOPLE WHO MADE ALL THE MONEY WERE THE ONES WHO SOLD SHOVELS, NOT THE ONES LOOKING FOR GOLD.

So, with that nugget of knowledge, I would suggest the person who is going to clean up here (Dad sort of joke) is whoever's selling bog paper.

* **SWEDISH PANCAKES** – Blodplättar (made from blood). Dad is a doofus because Harmony will find out at some point.

ADIOS, ALEESHAA.

I sent a text to Aleeshaa inviting her to come and watch **THE COOL** playing on the Beastival stage. And I offered her a backstage pass.

IS THAT, LIKE, THE MAIN STAGE?

was her reply.

THEY'VE ONLY GOT ONE . . .

was my 'curt' reply.

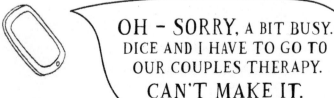

OH – SORRY, A BIT BUSY. DICE AND I HAVE TO GO TO OUR COUPLES THERAPY. CAN'T MAKE IT.

you might be wondering why I didn't mention to Aleeshaa that Bonio is playing with The Cool? Well, I'm smoking her out.

SHAME YOU CAN'T COME – BONIO IS PLAYING WITH THE COOL. **HOW DEADLY IS THAT?**

See how I outfoxed her there!

I have also been having to organise other things spit-spot. I've got Daffodil a small job helping out backstage making mint tea for the talent, but unfortunately there was no role for Felicity Snoop in that department. She'll just have to rock up with her pony like all the others in FRONT of the stage.

So I suppose this will be the moment me and Daffodil become **OFFICIAL** best countryside friends (OBCF's) again. But don't think I've forgotten Vinnie – even after his behaviour in Volume I and on the Mabel 'ratting to Grandpa' front.

Because I am the forgiving type, Vinnie has been rewarded by me with a contract to be a roadie. What that means is that he's in charge of Bonio's spare shoes and safety glasses. There's a whole flipping double-whopper van full of them under Vinnie's watchful eye.

SOCIAL-MEDIA NEWS

Harmony has just flipping well told me that Aleeshaa is saying stuff ALL OVER social media about Beastival and Bonio, and she's bigging herself up by telling everyone she's going to be backstage.

Aleeshaa is now officially banned from all THE COOL performances – for life.

I sent her a text from my lawyer.

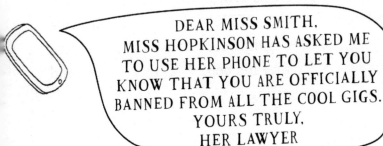

DEAR MISS SMITH,
MISS HOPKINSON HAS ASKED ME
TO USE HER PHONE TO LET YOU
KNOW THAT YOU ARE OFFICIALLY
BANNED FROM ALL THE COOL GIGS.
YOURS TRULY,
HER LAWYER

As far as Aleeshaa is concerned, it's no more Mr Nice Guy from Holly Hopkinson (schoolfriend). But I'm not going to 'Block This Caller' on my smart mobile phone cos I want to read her begging text messages!! As far as I'm concerned, she can just worry about rolling her Dice – cos I'm done with that girl.

Aleeshaa isn't the only person who will not be attending Beastival backstage this year – that rat from the *Daily Chipping Topley Mail* will find his press accreditation has been cancelled when he gets to the straw bales where the press passes are handed out.

The Gâllèrie de Muséé du Crêdules and my **MAGIC POCKET WATCH** have also successfully persuaded Vince to ban plastic bottles (as well as the cups) from the site in case there are any fish coming. It's bad enough that they have to swim their way through that stuff in the ocean, let alone wade through it on Vince's farm when they're already up to the gills in mud.

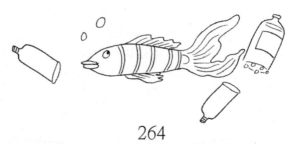

it looks like Vince has massively underestimated how many people are taking advantage of the FREE TICKET offer if you bring an animal with you. And you only have to take one look at Grandpa's farmyard to know what's going to happen.

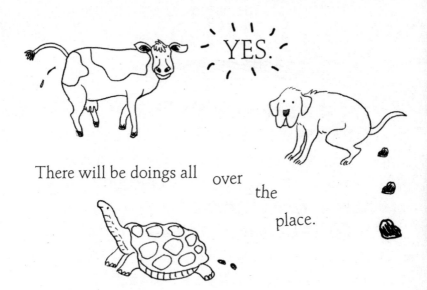

YES.

There will be doings all over the place.

CHAPTER 40

BONIO OFFICIALLY OPENS THE GÂLLÈRIE DE MUSÉÉ DU CRÊDULES' PICTURE INSTALLATION

THE MOST POPULAR EXTRAVAGANZA AT BEASTIVAL DURING THE AFTERNOON WAS BONIO OPENING THE DISPLAY OF GRANDPA'S PICTURES – ALTHOUGH I'M BEING GENEROUS HERE COS I SHOULD OFFICIALLY BE REFERRING TO IT AS THE GÂLLÈRIE DE MUSÉÉ DU CRÊDULES' PICTURE INSTALLATION, IF WE'RE GOING TO STICK TO OFFICIAL STUFF.

But Grandpa looks very happy and that is all that matters – I don't think he enjoyed pretending to be a farmer much.

Bonio stood on one of the tractor engines to officially declare the 'picture installation officially open'.

> 'LADIES AND GENTLEMEN, THIS IS THE GREATEST LIVING ARTIST ALIVE IN THE WORLD, AND I'VE FOUND HIM. WE ARE GOING TO TAKE THESE PICTURES ON A WORLD TOUR SO EVERYONE CAN GET TO APPRECIATE THIS GREAT TALENT!'

Bonio roared as he clapped and jumped up and down. You can see why he needs so many spare shoes.

Then Grandpa got some dust in his eyes and had to dab them with the corner of his neck handkerchief.

Everyone HOOTED and HOLLERED and made good animal noises, and Grandpa looked terrifically pleased. Well, everyone except Holly Hopkinson (Art Gallery Impresso Inc.).

267

'Excuse you,' I said to myself in my 'furious, absolutely furious' voice. 'Back up there a minute. No one has said anything to the Gâllèrie de Muséé du Crêdules about bunking off on a world tour, thank you very much. My **MAGIC POCKET WATCH** is going to be getting busy when everyone has calmed down.'

That's the flipping trouble with adults – one minute you think you've got them trained, and the next minute they've eaten too much sugar and spit-spot spun

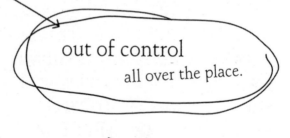

out of control
all over the place.

CHAPTER 41

THE CAPPA-CHINO WAR AND OTHER TROUBLE

THINGS GOT NASTY DURING THE AFTERNOON IN THE BEVERAGE AREA. MUM WAS UNDER THE IMPRESSION THAT SHE WOULD BE THE SOLE VENDOR OF COFFEE. SHE SAID I'D ORGANISED THAT – BUT, SEEING AS I DON'T SEE ANY APPLE MAC ARRIVING FROM THE AMAZON, I DO NOT THINK THAT DEAL WAS HONOURED BY MUM.

Aunt Electra says that Vince has sold her the exclusive rights to sell flat lattes – and she has a point there because my SPIRo, SPERo with Vince only covered cappa-chinos on Mum's behalf.

Then some chancer turned up and tried to start selling mucky-atos – well, Vinnie had him towed out of there before anyone could say Buenas Noches, Barista.

Mum and Aunt Electra are now circling each other like double-whopper SUMO WRESTLERS. One of them is going to get an ecofriendly mortal wound from a disposable coffee stirrer – and, by the time the coppers break through the new Olde Worlde housing people's protest, the offending weapon will have biodegraded and been composted.

I MAY BE GIVING **SERIOUS** VILLAINS OF THE FUTURE IDEAS HERE.

MORE BAD NEWS

Just when I was in a right flipping double-whopper state before Bonio and The Cool went onstage, I got a very unwelcome tap on the shoulder from Vinnie, who was having a busy day.

'See ova yonder?' Vinnie asked in his 'roadie' voice.

'Yorkel,' I replied in our secret Bogey Club language.

There was a very square-shaped man with dark glasses and a big hat standing with his feet apart outside Grandpa's 'pictures installation' tent.

''E's lookin' for you.'

'What does he want? Don't tell me – a backstage pass for The Cool's session.'

''E says one of the paintings in the tent's 'is. The orange one . . .'

> '**WHAAAT?** DON'T BE RIDICULOUS, VINNIE.'

But Vinnie had a determined look in his eye.

''Ere,' he said, flourishing a business card at me.

My blood went cold when I read it – and my stomach felt like I'd swallowed a double-whopper helping of Kiviak.

This was NOT **GOOD NEWS**.

LOFTY GAMBINO
PRIVATE INVESTIGATOR AND UNDERTAKER

'Vinnie . . . I don't really have time to discuss business matters with Mr Gambino right now. Is there any way you could make him disappear?*

'Yorkel,' Vinnie replied with his 'no-nonsense' face on.

'Thank you, Vinnie. I shall pretend we never had this conversation. I shall never return to it . . . you're on your own, Vinnie.'

'YORKEL.'

Vinnie is a reliable soul in certain areas –
I'm sure you get by now why he's still on the
waiting list to be appointed my official animal

best friend.

* **DISAPPEAR** – unofficial sources haven't
confirmed that Vinnie and three large, snarling
sheepdogs weren't seen shepherding a very
square-looking man into the back of Bonio's van.

The same sources haven't confirmed that the next
time the back of the van will be opened will be
in three weeks when Bonio does a gig in Istanbul.

CHAPTER 42

MISS BOSSOM GETS THE CROWD GOING

THE TENT NEXT TO GRANDPA'S PICTURE
INSTALLATION IS OFFICIALLY CALLED THE
ALTERNATIVE ENTERTAINMENT SUITE.
IT'S ACTUALLY A LARGE WIGWAM, AND
IT HAS A NASTY NIFF TO IT.

I authorised Vinnie to take some time off
roadie-ing, and he did his snail ventriloquist act.
With hindsight, it was probable that the Beastival
crowd would be quite rowdy – and, as WE
know from experience, Vinnie's snail,
Domino, is very shy.

Vinnie's act wasn't a great success, which is
probably a double-whopper good thing – cos he
needs to be concentrating on the jobs I'm going to
promote him to.

Sir Garfield, Dad's cricketing butcher friend, then did his ferret thing. I don't know what spooked the ferret, but the first-aid people said that Sir Garfield's injuries were not treatable 'on site'.

Hopefully he'll be back in time for The Cool's performance.

Then Miss Bossom came on, swaddled in veils like an Egyptian mummy. Her act looked like an escapologist trying to get undressed after wrapping up too warm. All the while shouting her head off quite out of tune.

But once she'd lost her top layers she spit-spot double-whopper made shapes that none of us were expecting – even in a WIGWAM.

Then I saw a guy in a suit looking very impressed, and I think he had a contract-looking piece of paper sticking out of his pocket. So at half-time I spit-spot bunked round to the back of the wigwam – if anyone is signing this **LUNATIC** up, it will be Holly Hopkinson (Band Manager Inc.).

Slinky Dave was standing at the back of the wigwam being the OFFICIAL bouncer and whiffing of aftershave.

'You won't believe the two geezers who've bin tryin' to get in 'ere,' Slinky Dave huffed. 'Tryin' to tell me they were Ed Shear'um and Andrew Lord Webber. What do they think I am – some kind of idiot?'

Alarm bells started ringing in my head.

'Er, Dave, what did they look like . . . exactly?'

'Hmm . . . I suppose they did look quite like Ed Shear'um and Andrew Lord Webber.'

DONNA KEBAB.

I now have two major celebrities wandering around and NOT under my supervision – they could be getting force-fed all sorts of food or being dragged into the Cappa-chino War.

Lower Goring could be about to hit the news headlines for the first time since Bossy's agricultural **wedding of the year.**

It will not be good for Holly Hopkinson (newly formed group of companies) to be associated with such associated dramas – so I flipping well need to find them double-whopper spit-spot fast before they end up in the fast-food chain.

CHAPTER 43

THE COOL ARE ON THE MAIN STAGE

ED SHEAR'UM AND ANDREW LORD WEBBER MAY NOT HAVE BLUFFED THEIR WAY PAST SLINKY DAVE, BUT THEY HAD SWANNED THEIR WAY INTO THE BACKSTAGE AREA BY THE TIME I SPIT-SPOT GOT THERE, TOTALLY OUT OF BREATH. AND THEY WERE QUAFFING DAFFODIL'S MINT TEA AS IF THEY WERE AT ONE OF THOSE BANQUETS DURING THE LAST DAYS OF THE ROMAN EMPIRE.

Of course I was as delighted as the next person that they were present – this will be the highlight of Holly Hopkinson's (Band Manager Inc.) career.

But I was also furious that Slinky Dave didn't know they were coming – so that I could control them for their own good and be seen hanging out with them – which is also good.

'Well, this IS a nice surprise,' I said in my 'Mum's fake' voice, but not forgetting to do a massive bow and courtesy to them, which got my knees covered in flipping mud. 'Brought any animals with you?'

'I've brought one of my cats,' Lord Andrew said. 'She's very keen on fast mice.'

'Well, she's come to the right place then,' I advised in my 'tour guide' voice. 'There's a whole flipping herd of them in the bins over there.'

And then I heard **massive** cheering from the crowd – and guess who'd got on the stage and was jazzing the crowd up, who were fermenting into a rightly flipping fever?

YES.

Vinnie – who was meant to be laying out some spare shoes for Bonio and a couple of pairs of safety glasses – but it had all gone to his head, and he was doing his funky chicken walk all over the stage.

I have never seen Vinnie

SO happy.

While the two big cheeses were watching him, I slipped into THE COOL'S changing gazebo and got my MAGIC POCKET WATCH out. (Bonio had his own separate pagoda specially shipped in from Chipping Topley; it's all right for some!)

It was time for a triple-witching SPIRO, SPERO session for my MAGIC POCKET WATCH.

'Guys . . . gather round . . . and look at my MAGIC POCKET WATCH.'

They all obeyed, and I gave them three rounds of SPIRO, SPERO, plus one for luck.

'You are The Cool,' I told them in my 'band manager's voice. 'And you are the greatest rock band in the world . . . but Bonio is OK too, so just do what he says and enjoy yourselves.'

They all nodded, and Shovel said, 'Nice one.'

And then the stage manager shouted for them, and it was Monte Carlo or Bust time. But there was no flipping sign of Bonio anywhere!

PINA DOLADO.

Ed Shear'um was up to his neck in mint tea and shooting the breeze with Daffodil – who was getting the hang of backstage super fast, thank you very much. So I had to go and knock on the flap of Bonio's pagoda.

'Excuse you, Bonio!' I shouted. 'It's show time . . . Let's go!'

Not a squeak – so I nipped inside to see if he was having a spit-spot power kip. But there was no double-whopper sign of him anywhere.

What the heck was going on? Then I heard a noise that sounded like a woolly mammoth sitting on a cold bog seat while eating one of Vera's cakes and drinking one of Aunt Electra's morning potions coming from his VIP BOG.

It was a terrible cacophony, as they say in Brazil during the CARNIVAL.

'Everything OK, Bonio?' I asked.

'Aaarrrggghhh . . . what was in that pancake?' Bonio groaned.

It didn't take me long to cross the dots and join up the T's and flipping well add two and two and get six*.

'Arrrggghhh . . . Oooouuufff . . . we'll have to call the gig off . . . my stomach's exploding.'

---

* SIX – I was right. My dad had slipped Bonio a flipping Blodplättar pancake stuffed with Kiviak.

HOLLY HOPKINSON (BAND MANAGER INC.)
DOES NOT CALL GIGS OFF,
THANK YOU
VERY MUCH,

so she had to expresso spit-spot find a switcheroo double-whopper fast.

And then *she* had a 'hey pesto bolt-from-Damascus' moment* – guess who came past, walking like a lunatic and looking like he could be a double for Bonio?

YES.

Vinnie.

So I fished out my **MAGIC POCKET WATCH** and got to work on him.

---

* 'HEY PESTO BOLT-FROM-DAMASCUS'
MOMENT – way too difficult to explain.

'Vinnie,' I said in my 'mystic' voice, 'you are going to impersonate Bonio . . . but do not try and do anything. Just make sure Harold, Stickly and the other DOOFUS know it's you and tell them to get on with it . . . do not play with any knobs or anything . . . and no funky chicken walk.'

'Yes, 'Olly.'

'Good boy . . . just wait a minute and I'll get Bonio's clothes off him.'

Bonio was busy making farmyard animal noises on his VIP BOG and was initially reluctant to chuck his clothes out – but some stern words straightened him out and the threat that I'd set Slinky Dave on him if he didn't cooperate.

Vinnie looked quite like Bonio in Bonio's special shoes and safety glasses – no one would guess it wasn't the ROCK LEGEND himself!

CHAPTER 44

SHOW TIME

BEASTIVAL WENT BONKERS WHEN
VINNIE WALKED ON TO THE STAGE
'FASHIONABLY LATE'. WHAT IS IT WITH
ADULTS? THE LONGER YOU KEEP THEM
WAITING, THE LOUDER THEY CHEER.

Obviously doing the entire crowd with my MAGIC POCKET WATCH was out of the question, but I did give a few of the backstage crew a couple of verses of SPIRO, SPERO and told them a wild animal had been locked in the VIP BOG (with the help of Bonio's belt) and should not be let out on any account.

Harold, Stickly and Shovel were delighted that all restrictions on their movements had been lifted, and they started to make a terrific noise – the loudest I've ever heard.

So loud in fact that people couldn't hear themselves think – which was a good thing.

Mum and Dad took time out from peddling their wares, and a ceasefire was called in the Cappachino War. Aunt Electra was right up at the front of the crowd in the mush pit, fluttering like a flag in a **HURRICANE**.

Then Harmony got in on the act and did a **BODY SURF** across the Mexican Morris dancers.

Grandpa put on a cool hat and some dark glasses so that he didn't get recognised by too many people when he came out of his tent. His celebrity walk has got much worse, and it's making Vera frown a lot. She is locked on to him now like a ballroom dancer. If she gets any closer, she'll be wearing the same pair of trousers.

Vince has never had so much food on his farm in his life; and he and Dad's cricketing butcher friend, Sir Garfield, who has made it back from the Chipping Topley Accident and Incident department, are doing their best to eat most of it.

The Cool started to step things up big time. Stickly was really making shapes and doing his stretches – Shovel started to charge round the stage like a bull in a Chinese shop, and Harold was whacking his drums like he was in the Charge of the Light Brigade.

The racket was bearably bad until Vinnie got hold of a flipping microphone. And then it occurred to me that I hadn't specifically told him not to sing.

Although it's stretching a point to call the noises that Vinnie pushed out singing – but the crowd didn't care. They were much more interested in Vinnie's trousers, which were falling down without a belt.

But, all things considered, this gig was a major step up from anything 'the lads' have done before – so I think Harold's dream of conquering both sides of the Atlantic is beginning to feel like it's on!

TWO THINGS TO NOTE:

1. Andrew Lord Webber drank so much mint tea, he was spit-spot bursting and didn't fancy a nature wee with all the animals that were wandering around. So he found the VIP BOG and unfortunately released a naked Bonio into the wild.

2. He streaked straight to his van and roared off at speed. He and Lofty Gambino are going to have a double-whopper very nasty surprise when they arrive in Istanbul.

EPILOGUE

SO THAT DOUBLE-WHOPPER SPIT-
SPOT WRAPS UP VOLUME III OF MY
MEMOIRS: AND I HAVE SURVIVED A
FEW MORE WEEKS ON GRANDPA'S FARM
ON THE OUTSKIRTS OF LOWER GORING.
BY THE SKIN OF MY PANTS.

It's been a flipping **TORRID** time, pardon my French, but somehow the Hopkinsons seem to have come out of it butter side up, and the world now looks set to be our LOBSTER.

Grandpa got such an amazing review in RoundaboutChippingTopley.com (my MAGIC POCKET WATCH may have played a small part in that) that art galleries around the world have gone DOUBLE-WHOPPER bonkers. So it looks like Holly Hopkinson (Art Gallery Impresso Inc.) and Grandpa may be bunking off on a POSH world tour. He says he needs to buy some new shoes because his new walk is giving him BLISTERS.

Dad and Aunt Electra have had some very good news too, thank you very much. As a result of one of those nosy-parker food critics surviving the free Blodplättar PANCAKES stuffed with Kiviak better than Bonio, they have been asked to go on a world tour 'to fascinate the palates of gourmets with TEMPTATIONS from around the globe'.

And Mum and Harmony will be hotting and totting too – cos they have been asked to set up a Vegan Arcade. That will also involve going on a world tour, to find some things to sell in the arcade, but they're going to go the opposite way round to Dad and Aunt Electra because the Hopkinson family values are NOT quite aligned on this one – and not even my flipping **MAGIC POCKET WATCH** can smooth that out – it's called a Khyber Impasse*. But they will probably want Holly Hopkinson (Fixing Agent Inc.) travelling with them in case Harmony reverts back to her protesting ways.

THE COOL were such a massive hit at Beastival that Andrew Lord Webber is thinking of signing them up (plus Vinnie) to go on a double-whopper spit-spot

WORLD TOUR.

The COOL

WORLD TOUR!

---

* KHYBER IMPASSE – when two groups of people travelling in opposite directions meet on a silk road, and neither of them will take their shoes off.

Whether he was consulted by my **MAGIC POCKET WATCH** before he considered such a doofus decision is TOP SECRET. Obviously Holly Hopkinson (Band Manager Inc.) will have to tour with them – which way round they go hasn't been decided.

Vinnie is cooking on gas and has now officially become a celebrity since his funky chicken walk at Beastival. I have rewarded him by finally making him officially my animal best friend.

He is planning on developing a few other walks and incorporating more words into his 'act'.

It will not come as a surprise to you that Vera has NOT been signed up to any world tour – not even one that involves the **DEMOLITION** of large buildings with cakes.

BEST FRIEND NEWS –

Daffodil, now my officially confirmed best friend in the world (urban and countryside) is going to accompany me on my world tours as my waiting lady because she still hasn't heard anything from the queen on that front. Her time with me can only improve her waiting skills.

This volume will now join the other two volumes in the (relocated) biscuit tin hidden by Vinnie and being guarded by Mabel.

Anyone not mentioned in my epilogue may regret not being my London best friend any more – THANK YOU VERY MUCH.

LAST FINAL NEWS –
HOT OFF THE FLIPPING PRESS
A COUPLE OF MINUTES AGO –

so I was in the kitchen and the landline phone rang – and, as usual, I was just first there, minding my own business.

'Holly Hopkinson,' I said in my 'helpful' voice. 'What can I do you for?'

'I wanna speak with Horatio,' said a woman in her 'American' voice. And no please or thank you, thank you very much.

'I'm sure you do, madam . . . join the flipping queue . . . halfway round Chipping Topley. Is it on a racing matter or a picture matter cos that involves different middle people?'

'I just wanna speak with Horatio,' squawked the noisy voice with no manners.

'Horatio Nelson? Well, you're a bit late . . . by a couple of hundred years actually.'

'No, Hopkinson . . . Who the heck are you anyways?'

'Excuse you, I am Mr Hopkinson's Executive Manager, thank you very much, and who the heck are you?'

Probably some kid from the village, I thought as Vera appeared with a **MENACING** look in her eye, carrying a hammer and chisel to deal with one of her cakes.

'It's Esme . . . Esme Hopkinson,' the phone squawked.

Well, my stomach turned into a Kiviak Blodplättar.

'Did you say half a pound of mince and a roast chicken?' I asked in my 'pretend' butcher's voice.

'Whaaat?' drawled the 'American' voice on the other end of the line.

'And we've got some nice sausages on offer,' I added.

'But I don't want any SAUSAGES . . . I wanna speak with Horatio Hopkinson.'

'Well, you've got the wrong number,' I replied. 'And good day to you, madam.'

The flipping phone rang again – and it was ANOTHER person using their 'American' voice.

'Can I speak to Sally Hopkinson?' the voice asked.

'NOT YOU AGAIN,'

I said.

'But we've only just placed this call, and I need to speak with Horatio Hopkinson. This is the Guggenheim Museum in New York on the line.'

'Of course it is . . . very funny,' I replied and put the phone down.

I think we'll have to change our number to stop these joke calls.

ADIOS.

PS I can hear those footsteps in the attic again, and they're picking up speed. Harold is staying over with Stickly tonight – which means it isn't him.